DEATH
BY THE
BOOK

BOOKS BY LUCY CONNELLY

DEATH
BY THE
BOOK

Lucy Connelly

bookouture

Published by Bookouture in 2024

An imprint of Storyfire Ltd.
Carmelite House
50 Victoria Embankment
London EC4Y 0DZ

www.bookouture.com

Storyfire Ltd's authorised representative in the EEA is Hachette Ireland
8 Castlecourt Centre
Castleknock Road
Castleknock
Dublin 15, D15 YF6A
Ireland

ISBN: 978-1-83525-719-7
eBook ISBN: 978-1-83525-718-0

To Scott Pierce, thank you for being my friend. You are missed.

'A house without books is like a body without a soul.'

Marcus Tullius Cicero

ONE

I'd never murdered someone with a stare, but I tried my best on author James Brandt. He'd insulted me for the third time since our panel began on the first day of the Shamrock Cove Literary Festival. We'd been talking about the difference between mystery and thrillers. I'd made the comment that some of my favorite books mixed genres.

James disagreed and then used my books as an example as to why that was a terrible idea. In fact, he was still blathering on about the quality of commercial reads, as in any book that actually sold more than a thousand copies, while I tried to kill him with a look.

Darn. He's still breathing.

While he was a somewhat popular writer on this side of the pond, especially here in Ireland, he didn't come close to my sales. Not that I would ever say that out loud.

But I could think it loudly.

I glanced over to my sister, Lizzie, who moderated the panel. Her hair was piled in a messy bun and wore a white blouse and pencil skirt that made her look like a librarian. Her eyebrows lifted, and she shot daggers at him with those piercing blue eyes of hers. My eyes were green, and I had a different hair color, but other than that, we were identical. I loved that my twin had my back. She always had been one of my champions in life, and in writing.

When he finally stopped talking, she looked at her watch. "Well, that's all we have time for right now," she said. "Let's give our panel a hand." It was a good ten minutes before we had to end, but she'd probably grown tired of him blathering on about his books being the only ones worth reading. I know I had.

Thunderous applause came from the crowd at the Shamrock Cove Library, one of the many stops for the literary festival my sister headed up. As the owner of the local bookstore, *Leabhair agus Seaniarsmaí*, which meant books and antiquities, she'd hoped to bring in new business. It had worked, but she hadn't realized the main guest speaker, James Brandt, was such a jerk. The literary committee had chosen him before she'd taken over, and he'd been nothing but a pain in the behind.

He wasn't happy about his accommodation in the quaint Shamrock Cottage, nor that his book signing was in the afternoon the next day. He preferred early signings.

I'd never met such a diva in my writer world, and that was saying something. I'd been an author for more than twenty years and I knew hundreds of writers.

He went to push past my sister, but she put a hand on his shoulder.

"Mr. Brandt, I'd appreciate it if you would be more respectful of your fellow authors during the festival. There is no reason to be so rude." My sister hated confrontation, and I was proud of her for saying something to the pompous jerk.

"I have no idea what you're going on about," he said. Then he pushed past her and left through the library's side door.

She sighed and shook her head.

"Hey, thanks for trying," I said.

She smirked. "He's lucky I didn't jump up and wring his

neck during the panel. What a toad. I can't believe he spoke like that about your books."

I shrugged. "I'm tough, I can take it." However, I couldn't believe we had nine more days of this. The Shamrock Cove Literary Festival prided itself on being one of the few events that ran for ten days. It was about nine days too many for me.

She grunted. "Right. That's why you were trying to kill him with your eyes."

"Kill who?" Lolly O'Malley, our neighbor on the court, asked. Her gray hair was in a ponytail, and she wore a violet-colored pantsuit. She always reminded me of one of the flowers in her garden. The court was in the bailey of a castle and contained six carefully maintained thatched cottages and luscious gardens behind a giant wall separating it from the rest of town. We inherited the home from our grandfather, a man we'd never known.

We lived at number three, and Lolly at number six. She was a grandmother to all and one of our favorite people in Shamrock Cove. The place and the people were kinder than we could have ever imagined. In the past few months, we'd grown to love everything about our new home in Ireland.

"No one, just a figure of speech," Lizzie covered.

"He was rather rude," Lolly said. She was in her seventies, and she had a quick mind. "Before we pick next year's authors we should do research into their personalities. I'll not have anyone besmirch our Mercy. He needed an ear-twisting, that eejit."

I smiled. "Thank you for that," I said. "But like I told my lovely sister, I can take it."

"You shouldn't have to," Lizzie said. "This is supposed to be a fun event. I should go to the cottage and talk with him."

I shook my head. "It will do no good," I said. "He isn't someone who will likely listen. It is impossible to negotiate with a narcissist. You'll just end up with both of you upset. Besides, it's over, and I don't have any more panels with him. We can let it go."

Lizzie pursed her lips. "Maybe you can let it go, but I'm not sure I can."

"Let's go get some lunch," I said as I glanced down at the piece of paper in my hand with the schedule. "That will make us all feel better."

Mr. Poe, our pup, yapped once from the floor. Black and fluffy, he was a clever little dude. And he never missed a chance for a meal. "See. Mr. Poe agrees. Besides, you only have an hour and a half before the next book signing at your shop," I reminded my sister.

There was no way I'd let her face that lion alone. James Brandt would eat her alive, and he wasn't worth our time.

Later that night, we were exhausted when we finally made it back to number three, our cottage. We'd just opened the front door and turned on the lights when they buzzed out.

"What happened?" Lizzie asked.

"Lights are out," I said.

She snorted. "Obviously. Check and see if it's just us. I paid the bill. At least, I think I did. I've been very busy." She turned on the flashlight on her phone.

"I'm certain you did," I said. "I'll check, though."

Even though it was drizzling rain, which was normal weather here in Ireland in the spring, I stepped outside. Our next-door neighbor, Scott, was on his porch. He was a computer programmer. He and his partner, Rob, had become great friends.

"Are your lights out too?" I asked. Though it was easy enough to tell. I could barely see him through the darkness of the court.

"Yes," he said. "I was just coming over to see if you were going through the same."

"We are."

"Ah, well. They'll be back up soon. My guess is the influx of attendees has put a strain on our resources. This usually happens a couple of times during the summer in the height of the season, but it never lasts for long."

Even as he said it, the lights flickered back on.

"There you go," he said. "Good night, Mercy."

"Night."

It had been a long day of being on my best behavior for fans. I needed some rest.

The next day, I'd just finished signing books at the bookstore when a blonde woman teetering on high heels stomped up to the table.

"Why are you still here?" she asked.

Rude.

"I've just finished my signing."

"Well, my client's signing is in an hour, and I have to get everything situated before he arrives. I need you to vacate the table as quickly as possible and take your books with you."

I cleared my throat. "Let me guess, you're James Brandt's agent?" It was funny how rude people sometimes came in pairs.

"Yes. Now, please, I have to hurry. Where is the woman who runs the shop? She really should be on top of things. The table should have been cleared twenty minutes ago. I gave her explicit instructions."

"That woman is my sister. And she is on top of things," I said. "We promised the fans we'd sign every book. It's part of what makes the festival stand out—the access to authors, and James is not the only author here."

Her jaw set hard. "But he is the guest of honor and the most important author here." She shoved the five books left on the table toward me.

I picked them up as Lizzie hurried over.

"Is James here yet? We're running behind," she said.

"He'll be here any minute," the woman said. "Which is why I need her to move quickly."

Lizzie took the books from me. "You must be Sebrena Walker, his agent. Let me put these up, and I'll grab the ones we have for James. There's already a queue outside the store waiting for him to sign their books."

"He won't sign for more than an hour. I suggest you hurry," Sebrena said.

"Can you go help Caro with the register?" Lizzie asked me. "I'm going to help set up here." She spoke politely, but I could tell from her frown that the woman was getting on her nerves.

"Are you sure? I don't mind saying something to her," I whispered the words.

She shook her head. "I'm fine," she whispered back.

I nodded. Saying what I thought would cause my sister stress, and that was the last thing she needed. I bit my lip and headed to the front of the bookstore.

About twenty minutes before the signing was to begin, the guest of honor still hadn't arrived.

Sebrena was on her phone and pointing at my sister.

I went to see what was going on.

"What's up?" I asked Lizzie.

"James was supposed to be here fifteen minutes ago. Sebrena hasn't been able to get him on the phone, and he's ignoring her texts."

Sebrena put her phone in the pocket of her pale-pink suit. Her teased blonde hair reminded me of some women back in Texas, who wore it in a fashion that was reminiscent of the seventies. "I'll need you to go and fetch him," she said. "I still need to make certain everything is in order here."

I opened my mouth to tell her she should *fetch* him, but Lizzie shook her head. She had that crease between her eyes that shows she was annoyed.

"Will you come with me?" she asked. I was exhausted. Signings drained me because it was a lot of people-ing for my introverted soul. I preferred staying home and wearing yoga pants, oversized sweatshirts, and writing alone in my office. But I could never say no to my sister.

Besides, James wasn't kind, and I was protective. My sister had been through so much trauma over the last year, and I did my best to make things easier for her. That included moving us to Ireland several months ago. But that had been one of the best decisions of our lives.

Except for that one time when we'd had a run-in with a murderer. But other than that, we'd had an idyllic existence in our new home.

I sighed and then nodded.

A few minutes later, we, along with Mr. Poe, were in my SUV. The vehicle stayed parked in front of the bookstore, as we had no parking on the court. I put the car in drive, and headed up to the cliffs of Shamrock Cove, towards where James's cottage sat.

The town was full of stone and brightly painted buildings that ended at the cliffs looking out to the sea. I'd never been to a more beautiful place, and I'd traveled quite a lot.

Along the cliffs, brightly colored summer cottages had been built to take advantage of the amazing sea views.

While James had complained about the accommodation, the quaint stone house with a beautiful garden and window boxes overlooked the sea and was very sought after. It was like something out of a fairy tale.

"It's so charming," Lizzie said. "How could he not love it here?"

"It is, and he's a grump. I doubt he'd be happy in a five-star hotel with every amenity one could imagine. He's just the type who likes to argue and complain." It hadn't taken much time in his presence to sum up the man. He was egotistical, self-important, and a narcissist. There was no way he would have been happy with anything the festival committee had done for him.

"Are you okay? I feel like this whole event has been extremely stressful for you," I said softly.

She shrugged. "It's also been fun, except for dealing with this guy and his agent. And we're way ahead as far as sales go. I was worried about how the store would make it until the summer tourist season, but we've done well the last few days. So, it's worth dealing with a few annoying people."

"Except this guy goes far beyond just annoying."

She laughed. "We will not be asking him back. Lolly made that very clear last night during our updates meeting."

I smiled. I adored Lolly.

We walked up to the arched front door, and then Lizzie knocked.

There was no answer.

She knocked again.

Nothing.

"Mr. Brandt? It's Lizzie McCarthy from the festival. I've come to take you to your book signing."

Nothing but birdsong around us. Even in late May, the wind off the sea chilled us. We shivered at the same time. I was in my writer leaves the house uniform, which consisted of dark jeans, a white blouse and black blazer. My sister wore a cardigan set.

"Do you think he already left, and we missed him?" she asked. "Maybe he's in town somewhere."

"His car is still here." I pointed to the Mercedes. "And we didn't pass anyone on the way up here."

"He could have walked."

Mr. Poe whined and scratched at the door. Then he looked at me expectantly. He was worried about something. Over the last few months, we had discovered he was quite an intuitive dog. That had come in useful, especially with Lizzie. He'd simply helped her through the dark times by being adorable and cuddling her when she needed him most.

Lizzie's panic attacks, which had been frequent before arriving in Ireland, were almost non-existent these days because of Mr. Poe.

I loved the little furball and was grateful to him for always looking after Lizzie. It was as if he understood what she was going through.

"I'll try the door," I said. I handed her his leash.

"But what if he's in there? Maybe he's getting dressed."

"Or he's asleep, and we need to wake him up."

She took a deep breath. "Okay."

I turned the brass knob in the center of the door, and it opened with a slow creak. Mr. Poe started to go inside.

"Stay," I said and then pointed at him.

He sighed but did as I asked. He really was the best dog.

I stepped inside and stopped.

Lizzie peeked over my shoulder. "Oh. No," she cried.

I didn't blame her. My stomach churned with dread and bile rose in my throat.

There under a bookcase, appearing to be very dead, was James Brandt.

TWO

After checking for a pulse and not finding one, I pulled my phone from my sweater pocket and dialed 999. It rang a few times, and then Kieran, our local detective inspector, answered.

"What did you do this time?" he joked, but I didn't think he'd be happy with the answer. While we had a bumpy start when Lizzie and I first arrived in Ireland months ago, he and I had been spending more time together. I called it research, but I'd become quite fond of the detective. And I think he felt the same about me, as he'd found my assistance with various cases helpful.

"We've found a body," I said.

Silence.

"You aren't playing games, are you?"

I cleared my throat. "Unfortunately, no. It's author James Brandt. It seems the bookshelf fell over on him. I checked for a pulse but didn't find one. There is a lot of blood around his head. My guess is that is how he died."

He sighed. "I'll be there in ten minutes. Wait outside and do not touch anything. I mean it. Do not try to investigate." There was an edge to his voice that hadn't been there before.

I sighed. He was just being protective of me and my sister, as well as his crime scene. "I know the drill."

"What did he say?" Lizzie asked from the doorway. She was pale and shivered even though the house was extremely warm.

"He said we should wait in the car for him. You go ahead. I'll be right there."

She frowned. "You aren't going snooping, are you? It's obvious how he died."

I shrugged. "I'm just going to have a look around."

"Mercy, no. I don't want Kieran tossing you in the slammer for being nosy."

I waved a hand at her. "Go on and sit in the car. I promise I won't be long. Besides, we're friends now. He's not going to throw me in jail."

Determined to keep my promise to her, I quickly glanced around the room. Two cups and saucers and a pot of long-chilled tea were on the table. Either he was messy, or he had a guest at some point for tea just before he died. On the table were two manuscripts. One had his name on it, but the other had no author or title.

I wanted to pick it up and look through it, but I couldn't risk adding my fingerprints.

I need to keep some gloves in my pocket. I pulled a tissue from my coat pocket but decided not to use it. I didn't want to risk rubbing off any potential prints.

The kitchen was tidy, and the kettle was cold. Whenever he'd died, it must have been a while ago.

The bedroom was tidy. There was nothing out of the ordinary in the house except for the dead man on the floor and the overturned bookcase.

It had probably been an accident. He'd been reaching for a book or something when the old bookcase tumbled over on him.

But there was a weird blue tinge around his mouth. That

could have meant he was poisoned, and a test would be needed to make certain.

After going through the small cottage again, I joined Lizzie in the car.

"What were you looking for?" she asked.

"Any signs of foul play," I said honestly. We didn't keep secrets from one another.

"Isn't it obvious how he died? That bookcase looked old and heavy."

I nodded. "It was. But it just seems odd and too on point."

"What?" She asked. "Death by books?"

"Exactly. At some point in the last twenty-four hours, he had a guest. There were two cups on the table, but the kettle was cold. There were also two manuscripts on the table as if he'd been going through them or, perhaps, showing them to someone."

"Well, Mercy, he was a writer. I know you're behind on the next book, but there are these things called manuscripts that writers are supposed to create."

"Ha. Very funny. Did Carrie text you again?" Carrie was my editor. While neither of them would ever admit it, she kept tabs on me through my sister. I pretended to be offended, but I thought it was kind of sweet. They were just looking out for me and had done since I'd moved to New York nearly fifteen years ago fresh out of college.

She shrugged.

"For the record, I'm not behind. She just wanted to see the first half of the book early. But after she shared an unfinished book with the marketing team the last time, I'm not sending her anything until I'm completely done."

Okay, the truth was I only had the first third. My excuse was I'd been busy helping my sister with the festival. I would finish on time, just as soon as all of this was over.

"If you say so," Lizzie said as if she didn't believe me.

A few minutes later, Detective Inspector Kieran O'Malley, and Sheila, his second in command, pulled into the drive of the cottage.

He wore a cable knit sweater and jeans. While I'd never say it out loud, he was quite handsome in a rugged sort of way.

I rolled down the window. "Stay in the car," he said. "I'll want to talk to you."

"He doesn't look happy with us," Mercy said.

"You're right about that, but it isn't our fault we found a dead body." And since I'd grown to know the detective inspector better, I understood how seriously he took the phrase serve and protect. He'd be worried about us finding a body in a place that very seldom saw any kind of crime.

Lizzie shivered. "I really need to get back to the bookstore. Poor Caro must be going crazy with all those people in line that are waiting for a dead man."

"Why don't you call her?" I suggested.

"And say what, that we found our guest of honor under a bookcase? I have a feeling Kieran wouldn't like that much."

I scrunched up my face. "You make a good point. But you need to let her know that he isn't coming. People were lined up outside waiting for him. Maybe say he's indisposed."

"I'll text her and tell her he won't be able to make it. That way, I don't have to answer the twenty questions that are bound to come if I call. I wonder if he died quickly," she said. She shuddered again. "Imagine if he didn't and then slowly being crushed by all those books. It's horrible."

It was. "He wasn't the nicest guy, but you're right. That would have been an awful way to die."

If that was really how he died. The bookcase was old, but he'd been a man in his early fifties who appeared healthy. He should have been able to at least slide out from underneath it if he'd been his usual unpleasant self.

That light blue around his lips made me wonder if there

had been some sort of foul play. As in maybe someone poisoned him first, and then, in a stupor, he'd pulled the bookcase down on himself.

At least, that's how my writer's brain would have composed the scene.

There was just one problem. James's death wasn't fiction. This wasn't the first time I'd found a dead body, but experience didn't make it any easier.

Kieran came back out. I pushed the button to roll down the window again.

"What were you doing here?" he asked. He held his notebook in his hand.

"We'd come to pick him up for his book signing at our shop," Lizzie offered.

"When he didn't answer, we tried the door. That's when we found him," I finished.

"Did you see or pass anyone on your way up the hill?"

"No," I said. "Why do you ask? It looks like he accidentally pulled the bookcase on top of himself."

"Right, but he had a guest. I was hoping you might identify who that was." He must have noticed the cups as well.

"We didn't see anyone as we came up to the cliffs," Lizzie said. "Do you know how long he's been lying like that?"

"That will be for the coroner to say," he said. "The forensic team is on the way."

"Forensics? So, you think something is not right about the scene?"

His eyebrows lifted. "I never said that. Sheila says he was a famous author but not as popular as you. I'm covering the bases, so my superiors know we've done our due diligence."

Had he paid me an offhand compliment about being popular? I hid my smile behind a fake cough. "That makes sense," I said. "What did you make of the two manuscripts on the table?"

"What do you mean? He was an author," he said.

"Right. Except one had his name on it, and the other didn't. Maybe he was looking over someone else's work to help them. Though..."

"What?" He gave me a glance that said, *spit it out.*

"He wasn't the nicest guy," I said honestly. "Like rude might be his middle name. I can't see him helping anyone but himself. I know how that sounds but he had quite the ego."

It wasn't kind to speak ill of the dead, but Kieran needed to know the truth. Lizzie and I had only spent a short time in James's presence and wanted to kill him. There was no telling how many others he'd offended with his behavior.

"And?"

"The paper of the manuscript appeared older than the other one. Like it had been stuck in a box for years. And I can't see him helping another author with their novel. He didn't seem the type to offer anyone assistance."

"You sound like you were not a fan," he said. Then he gave me that suspicious look. Not that he thought I'd hurt him, but that I knew more than I was telling.

"Don't go there," Lizzie said. "We were just sent to find him. We didn't kill him."

"He doesn't think that," I said. "Do you?"

"No. I don't think you killed him. I only want to make sure I have all the facts."

"You should talk to his agent if you think there is any reason to be suspicious. She was the one who sent us. If you ask me, she should have been the one to come pick him up, but she made an excuse and forced us to do it."

"What is her name?"

"Sebrena Walker," Lizzie said. "She wasn't very nice either."

"And where can I find her?"

"We left her at the bookshop. She was setting up for James's signing this afternoon."

"Can we leave now?" I asked. "Lizzie needs to get back to the store. With the literary festival going on, it is hectic."

"Do you think we should cancel the rest of the festival?" Lizzie asked. "I mean, our guest of honor is dead. It seems wrong to carry on. I should call the committee members. Can you tell me exactly what happened?"

"I can't help you with that. I can only say the investigation will be ongoing," he said. "I'll follow you to town. I need to speak with his agent and locate his next of kin. As for the future of the festival, you'll need to check with my grandmother. Though, I don't see any reason why you should end it. It is my understanding that you have several authors in attendance."

His walkie-talkie squawked. "Hold here for a moment. Let me speak to Sheila. I'll be right back."

We waited a few minutes.

"Follow me down the cliffs," he said when he came back out. Then he jumped into his cruiser, and we dutifully pulled in behind him. We had to park a few blocks away from the bookstore, as the street in front was now packed.

I turned to Lizzie. "Are you okay? This kind of stuff hits you harder than it does me. I can cover at the store if you need to be alone." She was still pale, and I worried she might be in shock.

While she'd become stronger over the last few months since we arrived in Ireland, she'd been through a lot the last year, including the deaths of our mother, Lizzie's fiancé, and his daughter. We'd left all that behind in the hopes that she could rebuild her life and get away from all of that grief. Not that it ever truly went away. At odd moments I'd find her staring out into the garden with sadness coating her person. It broke my heart.

Only in the last few weeks, while working on the festival, did she seem more like the positive, hopeful sister she'd always been.

"No. I'd rather be busy. Besides, don't you want to be there when Kieran interviews the agent? What if it wasn't an accident and she killed her client? From the outside, it appears they were two peas in a pod, but who knows?"

I smiled. She'd never admit it, but her curiosity had been piqued. In that way, we were the same.

I'd been wondering the same thing. Not that there was any reason to think murder. But it all felt very odd, and my gut said something was hinky about the situation. After the last time we'd solved a murder mystery, I'd learned to trust my gut.

"Okay, but just say the word if you need to go home and take a break."

"Noted."

Kieran waited at the door to the bookstore for us.

"Do you know when the signing will begin?" a woman dressed in all black asked. "We've been waiting quite a long time."

"The signing has been canceled," Kieran said. "We're going to have to ask you to please leave the area."

The crowd grumbled a fair amount. I didn't blame them. It was chilly, even for Shamrock Cove. They had been stuck outside for more than an hour.

"Several other panels and events are taking place," Lizzie added cheerfully. "Please check your schedules."

With that, Kieran ushered us inside.

"There you are," Caro said. Then she frowned. "Is he not with you?"

"Didn't you see my text?" Lizzie asked her.

She shook her head. "I've been busy on the checkout with customers. Why?"

There were several curious onlookers.

Lizzie went over to her and whispered something. Caro's eyes went wide.

"Where's his agent?" Kieran asked.

I pointed to the back of the store, where the signing table

was set up. She had stacked books and arranged them in several neat piles.

I felt sorry for her. The poor woman had no idea what was coming.

Unless she'd murdered her author.

THREE

Sebrena had a hand on her hip while the other arm held a stack of books. She stared at Kieran with an incredulous look as he told her what had happened to her client. Maybe she was in shock, but the narrowing of her eyes suggested she was angry.

"What are you talking about? I spoke to him last night. I don't know what you people are playing at, but I'm not fond of games."

Kieran crossed his arms and stared right back. "Mr. Brandt is dead, I assure you."

She frowned and set the books on the table. "Dead?" She blinked as if she'd heard the word for the first time. "I don't understand." She stumbled around the table and sat down hard in the chair.

I pretended to straighten books on a shelf close enough to hear what was being said, but not so close that Kieran would think I was being nosy.

Lizzie was at the register, helping clear the long line there, but she tapped a finger below her ear to ask if I might be listening.

I nodded.

"Ms. Walker, you said the last time you spoke to him was last night?" Kieran asked Sebrena.

"Uh, yes, last night. He called to see if I could find somewhere else for him to stay. He wasn't happy with the cottage they put him in, but everywhere was booked up. I'd offered to switch so he could stay in the B&B where I'm set up, but he said he needed more space."

"And did you speak to him today?"

"I texted his schedule to him this morning, and we were supposed to meet here for the signing and then to have dinner this evening. His publisher offered a new contract, and we needed to talk about it—he's really gone?" She shook her head as if she couldn't quite believe what she'd been told.

"Aye, he is. And did he answer your text this morning?"

She sighed. "Let me check." She rifled through her enormous tote bag and pulled out her phone.

"No, but that isn't unusual. He wasn't much of a texter. He was old-fashioned that way. I cannot believe he's gone. How did he die?"

"We're investigating," he said.

"Wait. Investigating. You think someone killed him?" Her eyes went wide. "He was not always the easiest man to get along with, but no one had any reason to murder him. He was quite beloved by his fans."

At least, by the ones who hadn't met him. Okay, that was mean. But I couldn't imagine anyone getting along with the angry man.

Kieran cleared his throat. "No one said anything about murder. It looks to be an accident, but I must follow up."

"Oh," she said. "Good. Though, if he were murdered, it might sell more books."

I can't believe she said that out loud.

Kieran's eyebrows popped up.

As if realizing how it sounded, she waved a hand. "I only

meant because he wrote thrillers. Even though he's gone, he does have an estate. As his agent, ensuring his books sell is still my job."

Wow. Again, I couldn't believe she'd said that out loud. She was as mercenary as they came. While she appeared shocked, she didn't necessarily act upset by the news. That made me suspicious.

If he has been murdered, she's at the top of my list.

"Right. Back to your dinner. Was the contract going to be good news or bad?"

"Well, good in a way," she said. "His last book didn't do as well as his others, so they were making the same sort of offer as the last one. He wouldn't have been happy that his advance didn't go up, but I managed to get some tours, and things worked into his contract to make up for that."

"Did he know his book hadn't done as well?"

I'd wondered about that.

She pursed her lips. "I—uh. No. I handle the business side of things. I didn't bother him with numbers or anything that might hinder his creativity. To be honest, he didn't want to know. As long as he received healthy advances and royalty checks, and he did, he didn't care."

Writing was a creative process, but I couldn't imagine not knowing the business side of things with my work. I'd kill Miranda, my agent, if she kept something like that from me.

"While we are making inquiries, I must ask if there was anyone who might want to cause him harm?"

She glanced up at me and glared.

Kieran followed her line of sight.

Oops. They caught me.

"Only other authors in the industry who might have been jealous of his success. Like I said, his fans adored him."

Kieran shook his head as he stared at me. "What about anyone from his past?"

She glanced down at her hands. "I'm afraid I couldn't say. I've been his agent for fifteen years, but we weren't that personally close the last few years. Like I said, I took care of the business side for him."

"Wait, you said the last few years. So, did you have a personal relationship with him before that?" Kieran had picked up on that as well. Good for him. I was curious about the answer.

"We were together for several years at the beginning of his writing career. But for the last ten or so it's only been a professional relationship. He was no longer interested in a personal relationship." She appeared embarrassed by this admission.

After they broke up, why had she stuck with him?

Money. Her commissions had to be more than decent. From her answers to Kieran's questions, it appeared that was what she cared most about.

"Did he have any family we should notify?"

She shook her head. "No. His parents died years ago. He quite often said he was an orphan and happy to be so."

That sounded like him.

"Right. I'll need you to stay in town until we finish our inquiries."

"No," she said.

"No?" Kieran's head snapped back as if she'd slapped him. It was almost comical.

"I'll need to head back to Dublin to make arrangements for his wake and memorial. I'll need to speak to his lawyer to find out what his last wishes might have been. Who else is there to do that?"

"Our inquiries shouldn't be more than a few days," he said. "I'm certain you can handle the necessary details from here until we are done."

She threw up her hands. "I do not understand why. The last thing I want is to be stuck here in this town."

"As I said, it's only until we complete our inquiries—a few days at most." His tone pretty much told her all she needed to hear. She wasn't going anywhere.

Her jaw set hard. "Fine."

He took down her information.

As she was leaving, she went to the counter. She motioned to Lizzie, and I moved closer.

"After what has happened, if your store returns a single one of James's books I'll make certain no author ever comes to sign here again." With that, she left.

"Great," Lizzie said. "Nothing like a threat to make the day brighter. We have over two hundred books for the signing, which isn't happening. I mean, it isn't his fault, but people won't be as eager to buy if they aren't autographed."

I shrugged. "Maybe they will be once it comes out that he's dead."

"Oh, that is all kinds of wrong," she said.

"I have to agree," Kieran said behind me.

"Better than Lizzie taking a loss because of James's accident," I said. "Thriller and mystery readers are a special breed when it comes to death. They may want his new book before it sells out. Plus, I'm not sure Sebrena has the power to cause trouble like that. I wouldn't worry about it, Lizzie."

There was definitely something nefarious about all of this, and I didn't like the fact that people might think my sister, or I, had something to do with it. Something didn't add up, and I needed to know the truth.

But was his death an accident? The blue tinge of his lips made me wonder. I couldn't seem to get the image out of my head.

That night, after the last author reading at the library, we'd been invited to Scott and Rob's house for dinner. Rob was a chef and was always trying out new recipes on us. They were as loving and caring as two friends could be, and we were incredibly lucky to be neighbors.

Rob had made Italian food tonight. He was a global chef, who pulled from his travels around the world for his inspiration. He was working on a cookbook, and we were the beneficiaries of his practicing each one to perfection.

Like always, the food was scrumptious. My sister was a wonderful cook, whereas I barely knew how to turn the stove top on to boil water.

Even Lizzie admitted Rob was on a whole different level when it came to cooking. We'd never been fed anything by him that we didn't absolutely love.

"Save room for cannolis," he said.

"Rob told me that the author who was mean to you yesterday during that panel died and that you guys were the ones who found him," Scott said.

Lizzie looked at me, and I shrugged.

I cleared my throat. "It's an ongoing investigation and we promised Kieran we wouldn't talk about it," I said.

"We also heard you guys killed him." Rob laughed. So, we knew he didn't take the rumors seriously.

"Not again," Lizzie groaned. She put her head in her hands. "If those kinds of rumors are going around, it will be terrible for the business. Not that it matters. A man has died. But we had nothing to do with it. Other than we found him."

It wasn't the first time people in the village had gossiped about us. There had been some murders on the court shortly after our arrival in Shamrock Cove. I did everything to prove our innocence, but it hadn't been easy. The killer had almost murdered me and Kieran.

"To be sure we know you didn't do it," Scott said. "We're just kidding."

"You have to swear you won't say anything," I said.

They made the sign of the cross.

"I'm only sharing so that you can set the rumors straight when you hear people talking about us. We found him crushed under a bookcase," I said. "And we have no idea how it happened. It could have been a terrible accident."

"There's something in your eyes." Rob pointed at me. "You don't think it was an accident." He already knew me too well.

I shrugged again. "We won't know until the coroner or medical examiner writes a report."

"Can you tell us more?"

Lizzie looked at me and shook her head, but these were our friends. The same ones who had looked out for us since we arrived.

"Swear again you won't say anything? This is not to be shared with anyone else."

They made the sign again and nodded.

"You saw how he acted yesterday. He wasn't the easiest person to get along with, and it looked like someone else had been in the house with him before he died."

I stopped before I gave them any details about the manuscripts or cups and saucers.

Their eyes grew large.

"So, murder?" Scott asked.

"There's no way to know," Lizzie said. "You've met my sister, the mystery writer. She's good at making up stories."

"Ouch," I said as her comment stung. Though, she was just trying to save me from Kieran's wrath if he found out we'd been sharing details. While I didn't care about myself, I wouldn't have people gossiping about my sweet sister. She didn't deserve that.

"I didn't mean it like that." Lizzie patted my hand. "It's just that you tend to think the worst of situations. The cottage is old, and perhaps the bookcase wasn't secured properly. There were a lot of heavy-looking books on it."

I pursed my lips. "True. But you have to admit he wasn't nice."

"There is that," Lizzie said. "Still. It is quite a reach to think he was murdered because he was so rude."

"The whole town is talking about him, so they are," Rob said. "When I was at the market this afternoon there were all kinds of rumors flying. Everything from that old cottage being haunted to he used to be a spy, and perhaps he'd been killed because of it."

I snorted. "A spy?"

Scott shrugged. "He did write complicated spy thrillers. A lot of those guys who write them tend to have been spies in real life."

"Those are just rumor," I said. "Most of those writers never actually admitted to being spies."

"Ian Fleming was," Scott said.

"True," I admitted.

"And I just watched *The Pigeon Tunnel* about John le Carré," Scott said. "There is a chance Brandt could have been a spy as well."

"You got me there. But just know that everyone who writes spy thrillers didn't necessarily come from that world. I don't know a lot about Brandt, but he would have bragged about that fact if it were true."

At least, maybe he would have. But then again, perhaps he had secrets. I couldn't stop thinking about the manuscripts on the table, one of which had no title or author. My brain went into overdrive.

Someone like James Brandt would have a title page on his work with his name on it. So, who did that manuscript belong to? I wished I could have taken a look at it.

"But we can't know for certain," Lizzie said. "Spies don't always admit what they once were."

I gave her a look.

"Well, it's true," she said. "It's certainly a better story than people thinking we killed him. Rob and Scott, feel free to spread that rumor instead."

They laughed.

"Consider it done," Rob said. "But you two will keep us informed as to what is really going on?"

"As much as we can without me getting in trouble with Kieran," I said. "Until we know exactly what happened, it isn't worth worrying about."

"There is something you aren't telling us," Scott said. "Something you found at the scene. You have that look in your eyes where your brain is working overtime."

"How do you know her so well, already?" Lizzie said.

We laughed.

"I promise that when it's okay with the good detective inspector to share, I will."

"I keep forgetting he got a promotion," Rob said.

"Have you thought any more about using Kieran as the lead for a new series?"

I'd had too much tequila one night and had admitted that I thought Kieran would make a fascinating lead. He'd worked with several different law agencies before settling down in the small town. I'd learned some things about his past. Enough to know he was well-respected among his colleagues.

Though, other than saying he needed a quieter life, he'd never told me the truth about why he'd moved home to Shamrock Cove.

"It's still rolling around in my brain." I pointed to my head. "But if you two ever tell him I said that, I will never forgive you."

They held up their hands in surrender. "What is said during tequila shots night, stays at tequila shots night."

This time we all laughed.

. . .

A few hours later, we headed home.

"The guys weren't wrong, you have been distracted all night," Lizzie said as we made our way down the path to our home.

"Something about the anonymous manuscript bothers me. Was he trying to use someone's work as his own? Or was he looking it over, and maybe the author didn't like what he had to say? We know how caustic he could be."

"True," Lizzie said. "But maybe he found the manuscript in the cottage and was reading it."

I nodded. "I wish I'd taken a better look."

"Maybe, if you're nice to Kieran, he'll let you look at it," she said. "Our favorite detective does seem to be sweet on you."

I laughed. "He thinks I'm too annoying for anything like that ever to happen," I said. Yes, we'd become friends, but we butted heads more often than not.

"And yet, he manages to make an excuse to come to the house a few times a week," Lizzie said. She smiled.

I waved a hand. "That's because you're always inviting him over and giving him coffee and baked goods. Maybe you're the one who is sweet on him."

She rolled her eyes. "Uh. No. We aren't going down that road any time soon. Besides, I'm usually left out while you two discuss different cases you've encountered.

"You should go to the station in the morning and talk to him," she said. "I bet he wouldn't mind some help."

Mr. Poe, who had been walking in front of us, yipped in agreement.

I gave a noncommittal shrug. She was right about the detective. When we'd first arrived, he wasn't happy about our interference in his case, but lately, he'd been more open about the ones he'd been working on and sometimes asked for my take.

But I had a feeling this was different. Lizzie and I were considered suspects because we'd found the body.

Still, it was worth a try.

I needed to see that manuscript. And I wanted to view the results of his tox screen.

My gut screamed that the cranky author had been poisoned.

FOUR

The next morning, I headed to the station to see if Kieran was there. Sheila was at the front desk and on the phone. I adored her. She spoke her mind, but was as kind as they came. Her red hair was piled on top of her head. At least, this week it was red. She changed it often, and didn't seem to care what people might think about it. Her attitude only made me like her more.

I waited while she finished the call.

"Mornin', Mercy. How can I help you?"

"Is Kieran in?"

"He's at the church dealing with the crowds," she said.

I pulled the schedule for the festival from my pocket. There was nothing at the church this morning.

"Crowds? I don't see anything going on there."

"Aye, some of that author's fans wanted to do some prayer vigil or something. They organized it overnight, but the crowds are staggering. No one suspected so many people could get here that fast. The priest called and asked for help managing the crowds trying to get into the church. Is there something I can do for you?"

"I was just curious about something to do with James's

death and had some questions for Kieran. Do you mind if I leave him a message?"

The phone rang again.

She picked it up but motioned me to head back toward the offices.

I smiled and waved.

As I'd hoped, boxes of evidence were stored around his office. The fourth one I opened had the manuscript on top. The paper was old and weathered, as if it had been around for at least twenty years or so. Not that I was an expert. I pulled out the gloves I'd stored in my pocket.

But before I began perusing, I stepped back into the hall to make sure Sheila was still on the phone.

She was, so I took out my cell. I photographed several pages of the novel without really looking at them. It was all about speed when I had to snoop like this.

Kieran may have given me access to the manuscript. Then again, maybe not. I skipped to the back to see if there was an acknowledgment page to give me some clue to the author.

There wasn't.

The End.

That was it.

I put the manuscript back and slipped off my gloves. Then, to cover my tracks, I scribbled a quick note to the detective inspector and left it on his desk. I asked him if they'd run a toxicology test and if there had been any poison in James's system. If there was, it might help us to understand why he would have pulled that bookshelf down on himself.

I wanted to get to the prayer vigil before it started, to take a look at who might be in attendance.

I did my best to ensure I replaced everything exactly where I'd found it. He wouldn't be happy if he discovered I'd been snooping. There wasn't time to go through the other boxes. I'd already been in his office too long.

Giving Sheila a quick wave as I went out the front door, I decided to head to the church at the top of the hill on Main Street to see what was happening.

Up the hill, Kieran and one of his men were waving people through a queue outside the church. Many of them were people from the festival who carried heavy bags full of books as they trudged inside.

I made my way around the queue to Kieran.

"Mornin'," he said. "Are you going to the service?"

I shook my head.

"I just left your office," I said. "I was hoping to get your opinion about something, but it can wait. Have you seen his agent, Sebrena?"

"She's inside preparing to speak. Why?"

I shrugged. "I was just hoping to talk to her."

He gave me the you-better-not-be-snooping eye. "About what? It better not be about my case?"

I rolled my eyes. "Of course not," I lied. I cleared my throat. "She mentioned something about all the books we had at the shop that were James's and she threatened Lizzie if she tried to return any of them. Threatened to have my sister blacklisted."

"Oh?" His eyebrows rose.

I nodded. "Yes. So, I wanted to ask her a question."

"And what's that?"

"Just if she had signed bookplates from James, we could put them in the novels." I made that up on the spot. I was kind of proud of myself.

"What's a bookplate?" He appeared confused.

"It's a sticker signed by the author that can go in the front of the books. If she had some, I thought it might help move some of the inventory at our store." I held up a hand. "And yes, I know how materialistic that sounds. I'm just trying to find a way to help Lizzie. She has hundreds of books to move."

"I see." But the look in his eyes was suspicious. He stared at me a few uncomfortable seconds but I wouldn't allow myself to squirm under this policeman's gaze.

Then he smirked. "Go around the side entrance and tell Danny I said to let you in. Last time I saw her, the agent was in one of those rooms off the side of the church. But I would not count on her hearing you out. She's in a mood."

"Thanks. I'll take my chances."

Well, that was easier than expected.

I did as he said, and Danny let me in. The inside of the church was cool and smelled of incense. I'd been in here for a few social events the town held, and it had a calming effect. Almost the same sort of feeling that I had when I first walked through the doors of Notre Dame in Paris.

I wasn't terribly religious, but I found old churches comforting in a way that I couldn't articulate. Lizzie joked that I'd probably been a nun in a past life, which made us laugh for hours afterward. I had nothing against nuns, I just had never had the faith necessary for that particular job.

After checking the first few rooms down the corridor, which were set up like classrooms, I found Sebrena in the restroom at the end of the long hall.

She slid some red lipstick on and then turned on me. Her hair was in a messy bun piled high on top of her head, and she wore a black suit with a red blouse. She reminded me of a Barbie with too much makeup.

"You're Mercy McCarthy," she said.

"Yes, we met yesterday at my sister's bookstore."

She frowned. "Did we? I don't remember. Everything is a blur from yesterday. I'm not sure I had my wits about me. Are you happy with your current agent? I'm certain I could get you better deals."

I blinked with surprise. *Wow.* She was all business. So much for feeling sorry for her dead client.

"I'm quite fond of Miranda, my agent. I came to talk about something else."

She frowned. "What's that?"

"You threatened my sister if she returned any of James's books to the warehouse."

Her eyebrows went up. "Did I? I think threatened is a strong word. I'm sure you misunderstood me, Ms. McCarthy."

"I don't think I did," I said. "But I have an idea for a way around it. A way that we could both benefit from."

"Oh? And what's that?" Since I'd turned down her offer to be my agent, her tone was as if she could barely stand the sight of me.

I pulled my shoulders back and stood taller. "Most authors have signed bookplates. I know I have to sign several thousand for each book that my publisher keeps on hand for special orders and events.

"If you have some, I thought we could use those for the books at the shop. The books would probably sell faster if they had his autograph. That way my sister could move the inventory quickly, and you'd benefit from those sales." I was aware of how mercenary that sounded, but she looked as if she were pondering the idea.

She lifted her chin and crossed her arms. "It just so happens I have thousands of them in my office," she said. "Like your publisher, I make him sign several hundred at a time with each new release. We use them as promotional items for his events when he is unable to attend."

"Well, if you could spare a couple hundred, it might be easier for Lizzie to move those books you were worried about. As some of the last books that are signed by the author, they would be quite valuable to fans. That way, nothing goes back to the warehouse."

It was cold to think that way, but also true.

She tapped a long, red nail against her chin. "I'll text my

assistant to ship them overnight. But I'll only give them to your sister if you agree to meet with me. Let me show you what my agency can do for you."

Wow. There were no words for the greediness of this woman. I had a feeling that poaching clients from other agencies was frowned upon in her business.

"Deal." I was only giving up some of my time to help my sister out. I could do that, at the very least.

"One more thing, you told the detective you'd talked to James the night before his death."

"I'm not sure how that is any business of yours," she said coldly.

I cleared my throat. "I'm not sure if you know, but my sister and I found him yesterday. Remember? You'd sent us to the cottage to pick him up when he hadn't shown at the bookstore?"

She frowned. "Did I? Again, I'm having trouble remembering all the details from yesterday. It's all still such a shock." The last sentence came off as if she'd been practicing it.

"Right. Anyway, when I was there, I noticed an older manuscript on the table. I was curious if you knew anything about it. Or why he might have it."

She frowned. "What do you mean?" She appeared genuinely confused.

"There were two manuscripts on the table. One, was the one he'd recently completed. The other was really old. I wondered if maybe he'd dug up an old story he'd written and was perhaps revising it. I wondered if maybe he'd said something to you."

That sounded better than suggesting he was plagiarizing someone's work.

"How do you know what things looked like in the cottage?"

Was she purposefully being obtuse?

"Like I said. I was there and before finding him, I'd noticed it." It didn't seem right to say I snooped after seeing the dead man.

"Yesterday seems ages ago. But I have no idea what you're talking about. He wouldn't go back to something old he'd written. He wanted nothing to do with the past. Said he couldn't stand to read his early work because he'd grown so much as a writer."

We had that in common. I cringed when I thought about some of my earlier books, even though they had sold well.

"Did you have a chance to see him yesterday before his, uh, accident?"

"Why do you care?" she asked suspiciously.

I shrugged. "He was a fellow author, and I was just curious. In a way, I hoped that his last day had been a good one." That too sounded plausible, though somewhat weak.

"Like I told the police officer. We spoke on the phone," she said. "He wasn't happy about his accommodation and wanted to find somewhere else to stay. Turns out he was on to something since that cottage killed him."

That was dramatic. From what I'd seen, it appeared he'd pulled the bookcase away from the wall. But why would he do that on purpose? That part, at least, had to have been an accident.

"He wasn't happy about being back here at all, but he said he had to put some of his demons to rest."

Wait. What?

"Back here?" And what demons?

"Didn't you know? That's why the literary society here hounded him to come home. He was born in Shamrock Cove, and his parents lived here for years."

That was news to me, and it made me wonder if there were skeletons in his closet.

"I had no idea." I followed her out of the restroom.

"That Lolly person from the festival committee talked him

into coming. He said she'd been good to him when he was a boy, and he couldn't keep telling her, no. She'd been asking him for years. Besides, he'd felt blocked the last few months and hoped coming back here might clear away some of the cobwebs from his past. Those were his exact words. And now look what happened. This town bloody killed him."

Father Donnelly, the priest at the church, rounded the corner. "Ms. Walker, we'll begin in five minutes."

"I'll be right there," she said.

Then she turned to me. "If you don't mind, I need some time to go over my notes for the service."

"Of course, thanks for your help."

"I'll have those bookplates shipped overnight to the bookshop. But I'd like to be there when the sale is happening."

Why? She seemed determined to make certain all of those books sold.

"I'll let Lizzie know."

I waited in the foyer of the church as people were being seated and then stood against the wall behind a pew toward the back. The church was packed.

The priest said a few words, and then Sebrena came out. She talked about James for twenty minutes, extolling his virtues. I was surprised she had so many good things to say about him.

From what I'd seen, he hadn't been the best of men, but she made him sound like a saint. The police believed his death had been an accident. But he'd come home to deal with his demons. The funny thing about demons was that they didn't always want to be sent along their way.

Maybe one of his demons had killed him.

FIVE

After James's service, I found Lolly seated in the front row. Since she'd known James as a boy, she could maybe give me some background. Though, I had to be careful. If I asked her anything too pointed, she'd tell her grandson, Kieran, and I'd be in trouble.

She was talking to Rob and Scott about something. Scott handed her a file folder, and she opened it.

"Hey, guys. I didn't expect to find you here," I said.

Rob shrugged. "The literary committee felt we needed to be here in support. You just missed Lizzie. She had to get back to the store."

"Well, it was nice of you to come," I said.

"We'll need to have a meeting of the court soon," Scott said.

"Why is that?" I asked.

He pointed to the file folder in Lolly's hand. "We have the names from the town lottery for house number one. We'll need to divide them up and vet them before we make a final decision."

Living where we did came with a great deal of responsibility, which the residents took quite seriously.

One had to inherit one of the homes to live on the court. If there were no heirs, then a lotto was held for Shamrock Cove residents. It was a way to keep the court full of people who cared deeply about the area and keeping up appearances with the gardens and the six homes in the castle's bailey.

It was like a homeowner's association on steroids but with way more restrictions. Living here came with a giant binder of rules, some of which we were still learning.

We'd inherited our house from a grandfather we'd never known. That said, every day we were here, Lizzie and I had grown more grateful to the man for leaving us our wonderful cottage and the bookshop. Yes, the restrictions were sometimes annoying, but I wouldn't have traded our neighbors for anyone.

House number one had been vacated and there were no heirs, so we had to choose the new owners from a lottery that was thrown for the Shamrock Cove residents.

The judge's home had been left to Lolly after he was murdered on his doorstep. She gave the house to her grandson Kieran, our local detective inspector. He'd moved in about a month ago.

"What do you mean by vet? I thought we just picked a name out of a hat like a real lotto."

They all smiled at me like I'd lost my mind.

"We take those who entered," Lolly said. "Then we vet them. The top five choices are then put in a hat, and we draw. We need to know they are the right fit for the court."

It wasn't as exclusive as she made it sound. The residents on the court came from all walks of life, but they had one thing in common. They believed in community and keeping things beautiful. Even I'd had to learn how to garden. And by garden, I meant mowing. My sister wouldn't allow me anywhere near the flowers.

"Well, just text us when you need us to do our bit, and

Lizzie and I will help," I said. "Lolly, I actually came over to ask you some questions. Can I walk you home?"

"That would be lovely, dear." Her Irish wolfhound, Bernard, waited for us just outside the door to the church. He was never far from her side.

The church was at the top of the hill on Main Street. From this high, the whole town, with its historic buildings and views of the roiling sea, looked like a picture postcard.

Once we were away from the crowds, she turned to me. "You're going to ask about James, aren't you? Because you're curious, and that eejit grandson of mine won't tell you anything."

I smiled. "It's like you know us both a little too well. I was curious, though. I had no idea James had been born here."

"Aye, he was. That was one of the draws of asking him to the festival. I knew his parents. His mother was a fine history professor at the university, and his father did something with medical research. Kept themselves to themselves. She did not want much to do with the community, except for being a part of the gardening club.

"I suppose she thought she was above it all. At least, that was the attitude I remember. I'm old, and I sometimes forget things, but I believe James went away to university in England, and I don't think he ever returned. He had a falling out with his father over something. At least that was the village gossip."

"Were his parents living here when they died?"

"No. His father, yes. But when he passed away some time ago, his mother moved back to Dublin. She died a few years later. They were both so young. Only in their sixties or so."

I smiled. Sixty was young to Lolly.

"Did he have any friends or anyone he was close to here?"

She shrugged. "He did. It's been some years, but he ran with a group of youngsters. Back then, I was taking care of my dear husband, who was quite ill. So, I did not know him well.

"You might ask the mayor. I believe they were in the same class for a while. I can say we'd asked for years for him to come as the guest of honor of our festival, and this was the first time he agreed. Full of himself, he was. Didn't care about helping out our wee community.

"And, aye, I know it isn't nice to speak ill of the dead, but he made everyone on the committee miserable, including your sister."

"Did he anger anyone enough for them to kill him?"

She frowned. "Now, why would you think that? Kieran says it was an accident. The bookshelf was as old as the cottage and fell on him. 'Tis terrible what happened. There's no need to go making trouble where there isn't any," she chastised.

I had to back off or she'd say something about my nosing around to her grandson.

I smiled. "I'm not. It just felt odd when I was at the scene." I told her about the extra cup and the manuscript.

"Well, he was a writer."

Everyone kept saying that. I needed to get home and look over the manuscript pages on my phone. I'd compare it with his other books. But an initial glance told me he didn't write it.

"Thanks for talking to me, Lolly."

"'Tis nothing. Anything else you need?"

"Several people from the festival and town attended the memorial service. Are you sure you can't think of anyone who may have been his friend?"

She shook her head. "I couldn't say. He was years behind my children and ahead of Kieran. But as far as I know, there was no reason for someone to kill him." She stopped. "Well..."

"What?"

"In his later teen years, he got into some trouble. I can't remember exactly but it was over a girl. He'd been accused of bullying a young girl. His parents threatened legal action against the school, and the matter was dropped. You'd have to ask Henry Charlton about that. He was headmaster back then.

"Again, though. Why stir up the past?"

"Let's say it's created an idea for a book," I said. It wasn't really a lie. I might never use true crime stories, but that didn't mean I couldn't be inspired by them. My instincts told me there was something wonky about his death. It was too on the nose that a bunch of books killed an author.

It made me think that someone was trying to make a point about James.

"Henry lives in the care facility down the street from the church," she said. "He's still sharp as a tack, but I do not know if he'll talk about one of his students. He likes to keep things close to the vest."

"I'll keep that in mind," I said.

Had James stirred up the past by coming to Shamrock Cove?

Maybe a grudge from long ago had been brought to the surface.

People had been murdered for less.

SIX

When I finished helping Lizzie with my duties at the festival, it was quite late in the afternoon. Talking to the headmaster would have to wait until another day. Lizzie and I were on the way home from the bookstore to change for the awards dinner, when her phone dinged.

She sighed.

"What is it?"

"The caterer is threatening to quit," she said.

"What's wrong?"

"He says Sebrena is demanding changes with the desserts. She wants James's favorite pudding served instead of the cake we'd decided on."

"She has no say, right? Just tell him to ignore her."

"I did. But she's standing over him, and he's threatening to leave. Dinner service begins in an hour. What am I going to do?"

"You go change. I'll see what I can do," I offered.

"It's my responsibility."

"Yes, but I speak literary agent."

"Are you sure?"

I nodded, already walking away.

I loved and protected my sister, and I would do anything to make sure she had the least amount of stress possible. However, it was her idea to join the festival committee. And the whole affair had been nothing but stress.

The awards dinner was at the community center across from the church at the top of the hill.

I had no idea why Sebrena thought she should have any sort of say on the menu that the committee had decided upon.

By the time I made it up the hill, I had to pause to catch my breath. The screaming coming from the back of the community center was difficult to ignore.

"Look, you harpy, get out of here, or I'll call the police," a male voice said.

Oh. My.

I went around the back and found a man in a chef's hat and apron pointing a finger at Sebrena.

"You're just being difficult because you're still jealous," she said.

He scoffed. "Trust me. I was over you the second you walked out the door and into the arms of that no-talent hack."

Wait. Had Sebrena and the chef been a couple? And was he now talking about James? I stepped back around the corner so they couldn't see me.

"Right. That's why you stalked me for a year."

"I've told you a million times I'd been hired to work that party. I wasn't stalking you. But none of that matters. You believe what you want. But you have no say in the menu the festival committee decided on."

"You just don't want to change things because it's me."

He grumbled something I couldn't hear. "Again, you have no say. Dinner service begins soon. Even if I had the necessary ingredients for your stupid pudding, there isn't time to make it. Go away."

"I won't. James deserves your respect. He was your friend."

The chef made a strange sound. "You've got to be kidding. I owed that man nothing. You, better than anyone must understand that. I heard he was threatening to leave your agency. You probably killed him so you could keep those gold-digging nails in his money."

"How dare you." She raised her hand to slap him, and I quickly stepped forward.

"Sebrena, I need to speak with you."

She bristled but turned. When she saw it was me, her frown turned into the fakest smile I'd ever seen.

"Yes? How can I help you, Ms. McCarthy."

"We thought it might be nice if I said a few words about James before the awards tonight. I was hoping you could help me with that."

"I—uh." She turned to speak to the chef, but he'd taken the distraction as an opportunity to sneak back inside. Smart man. Though their argument did make me wonder about their past.

Had he been talking about James when he mentioned the no-talent hack?

"Certainly. What do you need to know? Or it might be best if I were the one to say something, since I knew him best."

I nodded. "Right, though you spoke at the memorial, and everyone thought you might need a break. It's been a very emotional twenty-four hours for you."

She sighed and put the back of her hand to her forehead in a dramatic fashion. "That is true."

"It must be such a traumatic time for you, since you and the victim were together."

She waved a hand. "Oh, that was years ago. We hadn't been lovers for years. But I did leave my husband Patrick for James. I don't think he'll ever get over it. All I wanted was for him to make a special pudding to honor James, but he refused."

Husband. I hadn't expected that.

"I'm certain the committee insists on being very strict with the menu since they are serving so many," I said calmly. "You know, with all the dietary restrictions of the attendees."

The lies were rolling off my tongue. But I'd promised to take care of this for my sister.

"Still. There's time for adjustments," she said.

"Perhaps, like I mentioned, it would be better to honor him with words, since that was his thing."

She cocked her head. "That does make sense. Besides, Patrick is still so jealous there's no getting through to him."

Was he, though?

As mean as it might have sounded, I would have thought he dodged a bullet where Sebrena was concerned. The audacity that she could change the menu when she had nothing to do with the festival spoke loads to the type of woman she was.

However, jealousy was one of the main reasons for murder, and I didn't know Chef Patrick. Maybe he did still hold a torch for her. That gave me two strong suspects for my list.

But was that torch burning bright enough to commit murder?

"How long were you and Patrick married?"

"Almost three years," she said.

"That's a long time."

"There was a time when I thought he was the one. But his career was always more important than anyone in his life. That hasn't changed. He pretended to be heartbroken when I left him for James, but it was just because he was mad he'd lost one of his possessions. That was how he saw me."

Interesting.

She glanced at her phone worriedly.

"Is everything okay?"

"It's just the press," she said. "The publisher has asked that all comments go through them. They weren't happy I spoke at his memorial this morning—as if they could tell me what to do. I was his agent and his closest friend."

"Did James have any enemies?"

We'd been walking toward Main Street, and she paused. "What do you mean?"

"Was there anyone who might have wanted to cause him harm?"

She stared at me like I was crazy. "It was an accident, a terrible one. Why would you ask something like that?"

"Accidents could be staged," I said honestly.

"Wait. Do you think someone killed him? Impossible. He was a beloved author. I won't have you saying anything different about him."

"Oh, I'm not." I was. "I just want to ensure the police have covered all the bases."

"You mystery authors always think the worst," she said. "I suppose that is what makes you so good at your job."

I cleared my throat. "Thanks."

"As for enemies, he had a few. As I said, he was beloved by his fans. But sure, other authors were jealous of his success. You know how it is."

Most authors I knew were supportive, even the curmud-geonly ones I hung out with when I lived in Manhattan. It took a bit to earn their respect, but none of them had ever been as rude as James.

"Is there anyone in particular you'd say might have had it in for him?"

She shrugged. "Like I said, it was an accident. Why create drama where there is none?"

That was exactly what I would have said if I'd been the one to kill him. But what would have been her motive? Wasn't he worth more to her alive? Besides, that bookcase had been heavy, and she was a tiny woman.

Still, if he'd treated others the way he'd acted with my sister and me, he would have had more enemies than friends.

Then I remembered what he'd said about Sebrena having her claws in his finances. Maybe he'd been ready to make a move, and she put a stop to it. If he'd been poisoned, she could have done that.

Perhaps he was delirious from whatever poison she'd used, and accidentally pulled the bookcase down on himself.

No matter what she said, she was my number one suspect. No one else had been that close to James. I put Chef Patrick on there as well. Maybe he hadn't been as over their relationship as he'd claimed.

We sat at a table in the lobby of the cozy B&B where she was staying. I took some notes about his career from her—none of which I planned to use. I'd already texted my sister and told her I needed to give a small speech to cover my tracks.

Lizzie had texted back and said it was actually a good idea and would let the others know. I think she was just grateful I'd been able to pull Sebrena away from Chef Patrick.

As I took notes, my mind whirled. Could I be seated in front of a killer? She didn't seem the type to murder someone, but I would never be one to judge a book by its cover.

If James had been as problematic in the past as he had been at the festival, he probably had a trail of enemies. I wasn't the only author to have stalkers. Though, I'd hoped the worst of mine had stayed behind in New York. And so far, that person hadn't tried to hurt me—yet.

Maybe James had stalkers as well, and one of those enemies may have killed him.

SEVEN

The awards banquet was packed with festival attendees who had signed up to sit with their favorite authors at a table. Even though James was gone, several fans still sat at his table with Sebrena holding court. She smiled and talked nonstop.

Those at the table seemed to watch her as if she might be a bit off. Well, maybe more than a bit.

Lolly introduced the first speaker, who was the mayor. I'd met him a few times at various events. Like many politicians, he was a smooth talker, but it was difficult to believe anything he said about our little town being comparable to the capital city. The ones on this side of the pond weren't that different than their American counterparts.

He reminded me of those sports guys who peaked in high school or college and kept telling the same stories over and over.

The place had been decorated like a fairytale with ficus trees covered in twinkling lights. Flower garlands hung from the ceiling and walls, and candles lent a soft glow to the carefully decorated tables. It was all quite magical.

"Welcome to our Shamrock Cove Literary Awards Banquet," he said. "I'm Mayor Thomas Gilfoy. I want to take a moment to thank our extraordinary literary committee for hosting this auspicious event."

Everyone clapped.

"And to thank our many authors who have contributed their time to make this event a success."

There was more clapping and a few whistles. It was an enthusiastic crowd.

"It would be remiss of me not to mention our hometown hero, James Brandt, who will be much missed. I went to school with James, and he was a talented fellow." While he said positive words about the author, the mayor didn't sound or look enthusiastic, which made me think there may have been some bad blood there. He didn't have much of a poker face, which wasn't great for a politician.

I wondered if he'd been close to the author.

I put him on my mental list to talk to later.

He went on for a while, and then I heard my name. Lizzie gave me a soft elbow in the ribs. Everyone clapped, and I headed toward the stage. I wasn't much for public speaking, but it quite often came with the job. As long as I was prepared, and I was, everything was fine.

At least, that was what I told my stomach as nerves twisted it and made my throat dry.

"Good evening," I said. And then had to clear my throat. "Mayor Gilfoy is such a talented speaker, and he's a tough act to follow. Let's give him a hand."

There was a smattering of applause.

He smiled and nodded. I hoped some goodwill might get me an interview with him later.

"We often say writing isn't brain surgery," I said. "But it is psychology. A good writer knows why characters do things and the motivation behind their actions. For those who write mysteries and thrillers, it is essential that we understand why someone commits murder, and other crimes. At the same time, we must give the reader reasonable explanations and clues dropped along the way. It isn't always easy. But those winning awards this evening have done that and so much more. They've crafted wonderful tales that keep us guessing until the very end."

I paused for some applause.

"As the mayor said, we lost one of Ireland's great writers. The loss of James Brandt will be felt by the writing community here for years to come. Most of you are aware of his many accolades, so I won't repeat them here. I'm sure he took great comfort from his many fans who adored him. Let's raise a glass to your hometown hero, James Brandt."

Glasses were raised, and then everyone drank.

"Now on to our festivities for the night. Here to announce our first category is my sister, festival committee member, and bookstore owner, Lizzie McCarthy."

We hugged as she appeared on the stage, and I noticed her hands shaking.

"Take a deep breath," I said.

She smiled and nodded.

"I have the honor of announcing the winner of our thriller category," she said. The names of the nominees went up on a screen behind her. "As you know, festival attendees voted for each category. And the winner for thriller is..." She opened the envelope. "James Brandt."

People clapped politely.

"Accepting the award for James is his agent, Sebrena Walker."

Sebrena's red sequined dress was so tight I wasn't sure how she could move, or breathe, in it.

She took the award from my sister and put it on the podium. Then she pulled out several pages of paper.

This is going to be a long night.

"Our beloved James would have been so happy with this

great honor you have bestowed upon him," she said formally. "As you all know, he was taken far too soon by a tragedy. I knew when I met him many years ago..."

She went on for a full five minutes, talking about herself more than the author she represented. She'd done much the same at the church earlier in the day.

I noticed her squint as she looked toward the back of the room. I glanced behind me to find Chef Patrick, with his arms crossed, giving her the death stare.

He obviously hadn't forgotten their argument. He and Sebrena had been married for three years. It didn't matter how long ago they'd broken up. He still didn't like her very much.

Funnily enough, when I glanced at the mayor, he had the same look, as if he felt her words were distasteful.

Did the mayor have that much history with James? I'd have to ask.

By the time all eight awards had been announced, it was nearing nine p.m., and the attendees left quickly. Tomorrow, thankfully, was an easier day, but I had an early morning reading and needed my beauty sleep.

Still, I very much wanted to speak with the mayor. He seemed intent on escaping through the crowd as quickly as possible. I followed him outside, but he'd disappeared into the night.

Darn. Our chat would have to wait.

"Who are you looking for?" Kieran's voice made me jump.

"You have to stop sneaking up on me like that," I said.

He smiled, and my stomach flew into a kaleidoscope of butterflies.

"I came to find you," he said. "Did you win an award?"

I shook my head. "Since I was helping the committee, I recused myself from the competition."

"Ah."

"Is that what you wanted to know?"

"Nay. Why did you think we should do a tox screen on the author?"

I blinked, trying to think back to earlier when we'd found the body. I shrugged. "I don't know. The fact that he pulled the bookshelf on top of himself made me think maybe he'd been staggering or sick and reached out to steady himself. That and the two cups on the table. Someone had been there with him. And the bluish tinge around his mouth. Why?"

"I did have them run a tox screen. They haven't identified the toxin, but there was something in his system."

My eyes went wide. "So, he was poisoned?"

"Until they can identify it, which will be a few days, we can't be sure. We know there was something in his system that stopped his heart."

"Oh."

"Is there anything you'd like to share with me?" he asked. Then he stared at me pointedly.

"I'm not sure what you mean?"

"Well, you've been seen around town talking to various people. It's almost like you might be investigating, which I seem to remember you promising you wouldn't do."

I cleared my throat. "I didn't realize talking to people was against the law in Shamrock Cove. Is that in the court's housing book? I read it cover to cover, and I don't remember it saying that?"

"I thought if I were forthright with you, perhaps you'd be the same with me. You will investigate whether I want you to or not, so I thought perhaps we could share information to save time. And if we do, perhaps we can keep you out of harm's way."

I threw a hand against my chest. "You want my help? I feel faint," I joked.

He smirked. "So? Why don't we begin by you telling me what you've discovered so far."

"I learned earlier today that Sebrena was once married to the chef catering our events for the festival. And he was giving her the evil eye tonight during the awards ceremony. But that might have more to do with the fact that she was demanding he change part of the menu for tonight, which he, rightfully so, refused to do."

"And?"

"She left him for James. He mentioned a no-talent hack." I explained what I'd overheard.

Kieran's eyes widened with surprise. Maybe he hadn't made that connection yet. It made me happy that in some way I was able to help. And turn any sort of suspicion about my sister and me onto someone else.

"Okay. What else?"

"Evidently, the mayor knew James in school. He claims they were friends. But he didn't seem particularly broken up over his death. He too was staring daggers at Sebrena while she waxed poetic about James."

Kieran held up a hand. "Please, stay away from the mayor. The last thing I need is him filing charges against you for harassing him. I have a hard enough time with the man who constantly threatens my job."

I frowned. "That's awful. You're great at what you do."

"Says the woman who is constantly poking her nose into said job."

"I can't help it if I'm naturally curious."

He smirked and rolled his eyes.

"I haven't even had a chance to really talk to him," I said. At least, not yet. "I don't trust the agent. If I had to pinpoint a suspect in James's death, it would be her. They seemed at odds from what I heard. He made some not-so-nice comments about her during our panel.

"If she was about to lose him as a client, maybe she offed him before that could happen. You've seen how she acts. Everything is more about her than him."

"What else?"

"Well, that seems quite a lot. But I do plan to talk to the headmaster of James's old school, Henry Charlton. Your grandmother told me that he's in a care home, but I didn't have time to make it over there today."

"What would Henry know?"

I shrugged. "I was looking more for background on what kind of kid James might have been and if he left any sort of bad blood behind. There is no telling what he might have done when he was younger. And people have been known to hold grudges."

Kieran raised an eyebrow.

"Then there is the unidentified manuscript, which was about twenty years old, at least the paper looked like it. It's impossible for me to know for certain."

Except I had boxes of manuscripts back in New York, where I'd lived the last twenty years or so. Everything was in cold storage while I leased my apartment, but I'd kept every manuscript I'd written. And I knew paper.

"So you went through the manuscript?"

I cleared my throat. "I'm just going by what I saw at the cottage."

"What does the book have to do with anything?"

"Well, I have no idea," I said. "But from the quick glance I had when we found him, it didn't look like something he'd written. Or maybe he did write it a long time ago. I just found it odd that it was on the same table with his newest manuscript."

"How do you know it was his newest?" Kieran asked.

"The title page is the same as his next book. He mentioned it when we were on a panel the other night. He said it would be out next year. But why were they on the table together? And why were there two cups? Did he show the books to someone? Or had someone brought the older manuscript to see if James could get it published? That quite often happens to me. People want to give me their manuscripts to give to my agent or editor. Of course, I can't accept them. Nor would my agent or editor be open to reading something unsolicited. But writers can sometimes be pushy when it comes to their work. I just feel like that older manuscript means something. I'd like to read it through."

I let that hang in the air.

"If you'll wait and talk to Henry with me, I'll let you read it."

Progress. It was all I could do not to clap my hands. A few months ago, he would have told me to butt out. But over time we'd grown to trust one another enough to discuss just about everything to do with cases. My sister called our get-togethers dates. I found them informative research.

Then I eyed him suspiciously. "Why are you being so nice about me being nosy?"

"Because your nose is smart, and I came to find you to see what you could tell me about the older manuscript."

I smiled. "Oh."

"Stop by the station in the morning, and we'll go from there."

"Okay."

He started to walk away.

"Kieran?"

"Aye?" He turned toward me.

"You're thinking because of the toxin that we have a murder, aren't you?"

"Aye. But say nothing, and do not investigate on your own. We know how dangerous that can be. If you're curious about something, come to me first."

"Okay."

I may have blushed. His voice had a note of concern as if he were truly worried about my safety. We chatted as we headed down the hill, and parted when we reached the station.

"Promise you will keep your head down."

"I promise."

I headed home around the corner toward the court, but more than once I looked over my shoulder. I felt like someone was watching me.

When I turned, I didn't see anyone.

But I knew from previous experience that didn't necessarily mean someone wasn't there. I'd had my fair share of stalkers, one of whom had broken into my apartment on the Upper West Side in New York more than once.

One could never be too careful.

I shivered and hoped that the stalker in New York hadn't followed me to Shamrock Cove.

EIGHT

I woke up the following day with my face mashed down on my keyboard. When I was on deadline, that wasn't unusual. But I hadn't been working on my book. I'd done a deep dive on all things James Brandt. He'd been divorced three times and was in his fifties. Thanks to plastic surgery and hair plugs, he appeared slightly younger, but not by much.

His divorces had been acrimonious, with the women claiming he was emotionally abusive. I could see that. He was not the kindest of men and had a chip on his shoulder. I wondered how he convinced anyone to marry him. His three ex-wives went on my suspect list. At the very least, I could see if any of them had been in town or signed up for the festival.

The list was growing longer. Even though they had been friends I added the mayor to the list, with Sebrena and her ex, Chef Patrick. Victims usually knew their killers. Okay, so I didn't have any idea what the motivation for killing him might be—other than he wasn't very nice—but at least I had some people to check out.

Several gossipy articles about him were tied to various female celebrities.

He won a couple of court cases in which he was accused of plagiarism. That wasn't unusual for a top-selling author. It was one of the reasons I made things up rather than using true crimes as a basis for my stories.

I also took extra precautions. After I wrote each chapter, I emailed my drafts to myself as proof. No one could say after the fact that they'd come up with the same idea. So far, I've been lucky in that my books have never been challenged that way.

I'd written down a few things in my notebook, but at some point, in the early hours, I must have passed out. I glanced at my phone to see what time it was.

"Darn." I'd promised Lizzie I'd help her with the bookplates and crowds for James's posthumous signing.

After a quick shower, two cups of coffee, and a blueberry scone, I went to the bookstore. Instead of going around to Main Street, I went down the cobble-stone path behind the stores. I used my key to go into the back entrance and scared poor Lizzie to death as she was coming out of the office.

She dropped the pile of books she'd been carrying. We bent down to pick them up and bumped heads. We laughed. As identical twins, we often said or did things at the same time like some sort of hive mind.

We'd learned long ago to laugh at it.

"Sorry," I said. "I fell asleep last night and forgot to set an alarm."

"It's okay. Several of the committee members are here to help, and Lolly is barking orders like the commander-in-chief she is."

I laughed. Lolly was the grande dame of the court. Nothing in this village happened without her knowledge, and she had the respect of everyone in town.

I scooped up the books off the floor and handed them to Lizzie.

"How is it going?"

"It's weird," she said.

I frowned. "What do you mean?"

"Sebrena is acting like they're *her* books. I mean, not like she wrote them, but that she helped give James his ideas. We know that isn't true. You heard him on the panel. Most of his ideas were a meshing of true crime stories."

He had said exactly that. Like many authors, he felt it added authenticity to use old crime cases in his work. Popular murder cases were often used as a basis for fictional mystery or thriller novels. It was a way for many authors to feel their books were more authentic. He'd said this after I'd given a flippant, "I make things up" when asked where my stories came from by someone in the audience at the chat the other night.

He'd just wanted me to look like I was a worse writer than him, but he'd also been telling the truth. He often credited the cases in his acknowledgments.

"Maybe this is her fifteen minutes of fame," I said.

She shrugged. "I don't know, she's acting really weird. I've never seen anything like it."

"Tell me what I can do to help."

She handed me back the books I'd picked up off the floor. "Can you take these to the table, and I'll get another load? We're down to the last box, so it shouldn't be long before it's over."

"But you had hundreds."

She nodded. "It's been a very busy morning. I put a post on social media that we had the bookplates. It's the last chance for people to get autographed books from him, so the line was super long when we arrived this morning. Sebrena had James's assistant re-post what I said about this being the last chance for fans. It isn't just festival attendees who are here."

"Good. At least, you won't be stuck with all that inventory."

"I just hope James actually signed these bookplates," she

whispered. "I wouldn't put it past Sebrena to have forged his signature just to sell more novels."

"Yikes," I cringed. "Well, if she did, that's on her, not you. And I'm sorry. It was my idea to use the bookplates."

"No, don't get me wrong. I'm grateful to move the inventory. I didn't want to have to return them. But it's the way she's acting today, like she's taking ownership of all things James. Go see."

I headed down the hallway to find a long line snaking through the bookstore and out the front door.

"Would you like a picture?" Sebrena said to the next woman in line.

The woman appeared confused but nodded.

Sebrena held up one of James's books, and the woman took a selfie with her.

"Who is she?" the woman asked me as she walked away from the table.

It was all I could do not to laugh.

"James Brandt's agent, Sebrena Walker," I said as if that explained the agent's strange behavior.

"Ohhhh." But it was clear the woman still didn't understand why Sebrena acted the way she did.

Lolly and Scott were directing traffic in the store.

"Hi, Lolly, I'm here to help."

"You're a good lass," she said. "Can you check with your sister to see how many books we have left? Rob's going down the line to see how many readers we have. I don't want them waiting in line if we don't have any books to sell."

"Right. I'll check with Lizzie."

Lizzie put the books she'd been carrying on the table with Sebrena.

"Lolly sent me to find out how many books are left," I said.

"This is the last of them," she said.

I counted fifty-six. "Okay, I'll let her know."

Sebrena still had a large stack of signed bookplates in front of her. When she was busy with a fan, I snatched one and stuck it in my pocket. I planned on comparing the signature to one of the books James had signed for the auction happening later in the festival. I'd been there and witnessed him signing those books.

If Sebrena had forged them, it's not like I could do anything about it. I'd make my sister and the store look bad if I called her out. But I needed to know how far Sebrena would go to ensure James remained a bestseller. Her behavior was beyond suspicious.

Now that we knew James had some toxin in his system when he died, it would have been easy for her to poison him.

But why kill her cash cow?

Unless, he wasn't going to be hers for much longer. He'd been displeased with her about his accommodation for the trip. And more than once on the panel, he'd mentioned how his agent made sure she had her claws into everything he did.

Had he been thinking about switching agencies?

Her behavior was odd, but was she guilty of killing James? Money was often a great motivation for murder.

Then it hit me. Where was his laptop? I'd gone through the cottage before the police arrived and hadn't seen one. The older manuscript looked like it had been written on a typewriter years ago, but the newer one was clean and clearly straight off a printer.

James had been working on something new; he'd mentioned that during one of the panels. Maybe he didn't travel with his laptop, but that seemed unlikely to me. I was addicted to mine. My whole life was on there, and I seldom went anywhere without it. But James may have been different.

Or someone took it when they murdered him. But why?

My gut said it had to do with information. Someone didn't want him revealing something in his new book. At least, if I were writing a murder mystery, that would be the why of the story.

But this was a very real murder.

Sebrena was my prime suspect, given her odd behavior and penchant for greed.

"Aren't you Mercy McCarthy?" a woman asked.

I'd been staring down at my shoes and raised my head to find her gazing at me quizzically.

"I am."

"Is everything okay?"

I smiled. "Yes. Just making up stories in my head," I joked. "Can I help you with something?" She was about sixth in line for James's book.

"If it's not too much of an imposition, would you mind signing my books? I heard this was your sister's shop, and I was hoping I might see you. I was late getting here yesterday and missed your signing."

"Of course," I said.

She hauled a small crate loaded with books beside her. "I only have the first seven in the series with me. Can you sign them all?"

I smiled. I loved my fans so very much. I wrote because I loved to tell stories, but the bonus was that others enjoyed them as well. This made my week.

"Why don't you give them to me? I'll do that while you wait in line for James's book. Do you want them autographed or just signed?"

"Oh, these are for my keeper shelf. Can you sign them to Jill?"

"I'll do that."

She handed over the books and I took them back to Lizzie's office to sign them.

By the time I'd finished, she was up to the table where Sebrena handed her James's book.

"I'm sorry for your loss," Jill said. "He was a great writer."

Sebrena gave her a strained smile. "It was a great loss for us all. Do you want a selfie?"

Jill frowned. "Uh, no thanks."

Sebrena waved her away.

I handed her the autographed books. She grinned. "I'm so excited about meeting you. Thank you for signing all of these."

"No problem," I said. "Thank you for reading my books."

"Oh, I've read every word you've written. Through the years you've helped me get past some difficult times."

"I'm happy to hear that," I said. I was sure my cheeks had a blush on them, as my skin heated from the inside out.

"Can I take a selfie with you?" she asked me.

I nodded as Sebrena gave us the evil eye.

I was glad I'd thought to add makeup this morning, even though I'd been running late.

"Let me do that for you," Lizzie said as she came up behind Jill.

"Thank you," Jill said as she handed her the phone.

We took a couple of photos, and others in line asked if they could do the same.

Sebrena didn't seem to like me drawing attention away from her or James's books, but I didn't like disappointing people. Some authors would only sign books or take photos during signings or special events, and others made people pay for the privilege.

I was not one of those people. I was grateful for every reader who picked up one of my books, whether that was in a bookstore, on their e-reader, at the library, or listened to them. Reader generosity allowed me to live a life I could never have imagined when I first started out.

. . .

After I'd finished with the photos and signed a few more books, it was time for me to do my reading.

I had to race home for my tablet. Then, I headed to the community center, which was up the hill near the church. The place was packed as people streamed in, and I was surprised that there wasn't a single seat available.

The mayor was up at the front, talking with one of his assistants. He waved me over.

"I have the introduction ready, but is there anything you'd like me to add?" he asked. He was in his late fifties and dyed his hair black. He had a handlebar mustache and a long beard. He looked more like someone who hung out in SoHo or Greenwich Village back home rather than a small-town Irish mayor. However, his heavy Irish brogue was unmistakable, even if it sometimes made him difficult to understand.

"I'm sure whatever you have will be fine. Can I ask you something really quick?"

He glanced at his phone. We still had ten minutes before the event began.

"Yes," he said.

"Were you friends with James Brandt?"

"We ran with some of the same crowd," he said. "He was bookish, even back then."

"Would you say you were friends with him?"

He frowned. "Yes. Why do you ask?"

"I just found out he was from here, and I was curious why he never mentioned it. I noticed that it wasn't in his bio. We live in such a beautiful town, and I can't imagine why he wouldn't admit it."

The mayor rolled his eyes. "I think he was embarrassed about coming from such a small town," he said. "It took us forever to get him here for this event."

"Was it because he was a snob?"

The mayor's eyebrows went up. "No love lost between you, I see," he said.

"I didn't really know him," I said. "But I noticed he was somewhat abrupt and rude. Was he always that way?"

"Aye," he said. "That one always had a sharp tongue. When he went off for university, it was as if Shamrock Cove no longer existed."

"So, you didn't stay in touch?"

"We chatted at various events when I was in Dublin through the years. But we weren't particularly close anymore. When he left town, we weren't on the best of terms."

"Oh? Why was that?"

He bristled as if the memory made him angry.

"Fancied himself a ladies' man and thought nothing of dating anyone he wanted, even if the girl in question was with someone else."

So, this was a pattern.

Jealousy was a great reason for murder. Well, there was no good reason to kill someone. But jealousy was up there for the most popular motivations.

"He dated your girlfriend?"

"Aye," he said. "But I wasn't the only one."

"That must have made you very angry."

"At the time, I was young and immature, so yes. We had some words, and I may have given him a walloping."

"Mature or not, that wasn't a nice thing for him to do. I don't blame you for punching him."

"I shouldn't speak ill of the dead, but James was never a particularly nice or kind person. When I look back on our time together, I sometimes wonder why we ever became friends."

"Was he a writer back then?"

"Aye, he actually formed the literary club at school. We all fancied ourselves writers back then. That was how we all became mates. Though, I'd known him since primary school."

Something else to follow up on later. Maybe one of the members had written the other manuscript.

"Did he have any enemies other than those who he had stolen girlfriends from?"

"Enemies? I don't know if I'd go that far. Did he hurt some pride and deserve a bollocking? Yes. But I don't know that he had enemies. When he became famous, most people forgave his eccentricities of youth."

"And you were one of those people?"

He shrugged. "I might have married Sheila, if he hadn't taken her from me."

"Wait, Sheila, the police officer?"

He smiled. "Aye, that's the one. If we stayed together, I might never have become mayor."

"Why is that?"

He cleared his throat. "Let's just say she was wild back then, and I might have found myself in a wee bit of trouble."

"But she became an officer of the law. She couldn't have been that bad."

He shrugged. "Says you."

What did he mean by that?

I'd have to talk to Sheila. I had no idea she'd run in the mayor's circle back in the day. During her off hours, she was prone to wear older punk or rock star shirts and wasn't the prim and proper type. But she believed in law and order, and she was a great officer. Everyone in town adored her.

"Is there anyone who might have wanted him dead?"

He frowned. "Why would you ask that? 'Twas an accident."

"It's my author brain going crazy. Uh, I was just curious. Did you have time to go visit him at Shamrock Cottage?" I was determined to find out who his guest had been.

"No. I spoke with him after your panel, and then later we'd seen each other in the pub. He was killed by an accident with the bookcase. Are you putting that in the story you are working on?" He seemed genuinely curious.

"I may. The whole thing is rolling around in my mystery writer's brain," I said as if that explained everything. Evidently, the detective hadn't relayed the latest information about James ingesting some toxin to the mayor.

If James had been murdered, I was certain his agent was responsible for the author's death. Her behavior was strange and erratic. Proving it was another matter.

But I had to keep my options and mind open to other suspects. The more I learned about James and the people he ran around with in school, the more I wondered if the past had something to do with his death.

"Like I said, I wasn't the only one whose woman he stole, but that was all water under the bridge. And it was years ago. We're all past that now."

But were they? That kind of betrayal wasn't forgotten easily. It was just part of human nature to hold a grudge.

James had done the same thing with Sebrena, and then dumped her, even though she was still his agent. The anger between her and Chef Patrick was proof of how long hurt feelings could last.

"It's time," his assistant said.

The mayor headed to the podium.

He seemed cagey when I asked about the past.

Could he have killed James?

From what I'd learned about him over the last few months, the mayor wasn't the type to get his hands dirty.

But that didn't mean he couldn't hire someone else to do it.

NINE

After my reading, I had time to run by the station. Kieran had offered to let me look at the manuscript and I hoped he'd let me make a copy, so I didn't have to sit in the station to read it.

Main Street was crowded with visitors, and it was strange to see so many people in our small town. When we'd first arrived, it had been off season and wintry. Even though spring had arrived, it was chilly. But the masses of literary attendees made it appear like we'd been invaded in the middle of summer.

While I understood we were doing a great thing for literature, I preferred the quiet of our quaint little town.

It was funny how I'd already come to think of this place as home.

Sheila was on the phone at the front desk. "Hold, please," she said to the person on the line. She pointed to the back. "He's expecting you." She returned her attention to the phone. I wanted to ask her questions regarding what the mayor said.

If she had dated James, wouldn't that have been a conflict of interest if she was helping with the investigation?

Since Sheila was on the phone, I'd have to talk to her later.

I headed down the hallway to Kieran's office.

He, too, was on the phone, but he motioned for me to sit in one of the chairs in front of his desk. Like the rest of the buildings in Shamrock Cove, the police station was a couple hundred, maybe more, years old. The thatched cottage with bright floral wallpaper throughout wasn't like any law enforcement headquarters I'd ever been in. I'd been in plenty of precincts to do research. None had ever been what I'd call quaint or pretty, but the one here in Shamrock Cove was exactly that.

"Right, but can you tell me what kind of poison?"

He frowned.

"But when will you know? And could the hematoma have been caused by the falling bookcase? Right. Again, how much longer?" He sounded frustrated.

When he hung up, he sighed.

"What's wrong?" I asked.

"The postmortem is taking forever. They are understaffed in Dublin, and while they'd never admit it, outsiders like us are last in line."

"But James was quite famous. Not that that should matter, but at home it would. Celebrity puts people ahead."

"It's the same here. I have the mayor and my superiors in Dublin throwing questions right and left. They want the case tied up quickly. Which is why they've at least done part of the toxicology, but they still haven't narrowed down what type of poison it was. Every time I ask, it's another twenty-four hours."

"Do they at least know how he ingested it? Was it in the tea we saw on the table?"

"They can't say yet." He sighed and changed the subject. "Tell me what you've learned so far."

"Really?" This was quite the change. He normally didn't like my poking about. He claimed it was for my safety, but I wasn't always certain about that.

"Yes. You're good at looking at cases from a different angle than we might."

I think that might have been a compliment, but I wasn't about to say anything about it.

"Right. I've chatted with a few people. Like I told you last night, my time with Brandt was limited to the few events we did together at the festival."

"Okay. What can you tell me so far?"

"I believe there was a chance he was going to fire Sebrena as his agent. I have nothing to confirm this except what he said during our panels; that she had her claws in everything. He didn't seem very happy with her, though I'm not sure he understood the word happy."

Kieran nodded for me to continue.

I appreciated that he was taking me seriously.

"He also had a reputation for stealing women from other men." I told him about Sebrena and the chef who had been making our meals. And what I'd learned from the mayor.

"Did you know the mayor used to date Sheila?" I whispered the words so she wouldn't hear.

He laughed hard.

"What? It's true."

"I know it is. It was your face and the whisper. She didn't kill him. She was here at the station with me during the suspected murder window."

That was a relief. Not that I thought Sheila could do anything like that. I'd always liked her forthrightness and friendly demeanor.

"That said, they all had motive to murder him. He made a habit of stealing women from other men as if it were some game."

"But that was years ago," he said.

"Correct. But those are only the angry exes we know about. And it might have nothing to do with any of them. That's why

I'm here to see the manuscript. I was hoping you might allow me to make a copy so I can read it at home."

"Did you not get enough pictures when you were here?"

I blinked. How did he know? My throat dried and I probably had a deer in the headlight look. "What?"

He pointed his pen toward the ceiling, where there was a camera.

Oops. I'd missed that new addition.

"After the last time you broke into my office, I put a camera in to see what you were doing."

I bit my lip. *Well, that's embarrassing.* I'd been caught red-handed.

"Right. Have I mentioned how curious I am about things? It gets me into trouble all the time. But I didn't break in so much as make excuses so I could look into what you'd discovered so far."

"That's why I'm including you in the investigation. Hopefully, if I know what you are doing, I can keep you safe." His voice was kind, as if he really was worried about looking after me. An unfamiliar warmth spread through my chest. While my sister and mom had always looked out for me, it was different to have a man, especially one as handsome as Kieran, who cared.

Still, I didn't want to make too much of it. He just didn't want to have to investigate another murder because I'd stuck my nose where it didn't belong.

"Thanks. So, cards on the table. James was a bright man. I can't see him pulling a bookcase down on himself, accident or otherwise. The teacups and teapot were still on the table, and we had two manuscripts. One was for a book that is about to come out. And the other was written on a typewriter years ago. I'd say close to twenty from the color and type of paper."

"Again, how do you know that last bit?"

I shrugged. "I keep a hard copy of all my manuscripts. I just moved them into special boxes to help protect the paper before we moved here, so I remember seeing the paper from that time. There are tests your forensic folks can run to see for sure. I wondered if the older manuscript might have been something he wrote when he was younger. But why were they both on the table? I want to compare them."

"Do you think he plagiarized from someone? That could be a good motive."

I shrugged. "I wondered that and I read a few articles about court cases in which he was involved for plagiarism. But he'd won."

"Aye, we're looking into those who brought the cases against him."

"That's smart. Any time a writer's ego is involved, you never know how someone might react.

"I only had a chance to look at a few pages," I said. "I didn't see anything that would make me think that it was stolen. From the little I saw, it didn't even read like his writing. Even if it had been done years ago. But I need to read them through side by side."

He put two boxes of paper on his desk. "We made you copies. I cannot stress how much I need you to keep these under wraps. It would be my job if it was known we let evidence out of the building."

Part of me was secretly pleased that he knew me so well, and the other part was happy that, after all, he really did trust me.

"I am the soul of discretion."

He cocked his head. "You don't even share these with your sister. If I find out you've been telling the court about the investigation, I'll lock you out for good."

"Understood," I said. "I know Sheila didn't kill him, but have you spoken to her about him?" I had lowered my voice again when I said her name.

His eyes widened. "I told you. She was here at the station. You don't think one of my officers killed him, do you?"

I held up my hand. "No. I like Sheila, I just thought she might be able to give us some insight into the past. I feel like I'm missing a big piece of the puzzle from when he lived here. Everyone seems to have lost touch with him, and he seemed embarrassed that he'd come from such small-town life.

"So, why did he finally give in and come back to a town he was embarrassed about? Several people told me they'd been asking him to return for years. So why now? What changed? Maybe Sheila might have some insight."

"But I don't," she said from the doorway. "And I did not kill him."

I had a habit of sticking my foot into my mouth lately.

I attempted to swiftly backpedal. "Oh, I didn't think you did. But you knew him when he was younger, and you're a law officer. You have a different perspective, and I was hoping for some insight. Did you meet him at school?"

"I was a year below his crowd," she said. "But half the girls in the school wanted to date him."

"So how did you meet?"

"He was my maths tutor. You know how they say writers don't always do math? He did. He was brilliant and quite beautiful when he was younger. And he was kind to me. Unlike everyone else around me, he didn't make me feel dumb."

I was surprised to hear he was kind to her.

"When did you start dating?"

"Around my seventeenth birthday, but only for a month or so. It was embarrassing when he broke it off, and I had to find a new tutor. I'm still not great at maths, but he helped me to pass."

"Were you upset?"

"By the end, it was almost a relief to break up. I just didn't fit in with that crowd; I'd been dating the mayor before James, you see. The looks he gave us—well, I was just uncomfortable. I was such a babe, back then. When he lost interest, he didn't say anything about breaking up. He just ignored me completely. I wouldn't allow a man to ignore me like that now."

"Can you tell us about his inner circle? The mayor and the others."

She pursed her lips. "The only time they were all together when I was around was during football matches. Like I said, they did not bother with me much. I was just another girl James was dating. At first, James made fun of the mayor that he couldn't hold on to his women, which made him angry. They said a few words in my presence. But they were still friends long after we broke up."

"Was there anyone in that group you think might want to kill him?"

She shrugged. "I'm sure you've heard I wasn't the only girl he'd taken from another man. He did it so often everyone thought it was a game and that it was expected. I didn't realize then how I was being used as a part of his ego trip."

"Was he working on a manuscript in high school?"

She nodded. "He told me about a book he was working on back then. But it was so long ago, I can't tell you what it was about. He said it was fiction based on a true story about a girl their age who had gone missing. That's all I remember."

I glanced from her to Kieran.

Was the older manuscript the key to a mystery? One that someone didn't want others to find out about? And if it was based on a true story, who had gone missing?

"Is there anyone you think might have wanted him dead?"

Sheila ran a hand through her hair. "After we broke up, I avoided him and his friends. If I saw him, he usually had his arm wrapped around a new girl.

"He could be cruel. I remember people being genuinely afraid of him. Even then, he used words powerfully."

"Was there anyone specifically you can think of that he may have hurt in some way?"

"You'd be looking at a third of the people in secondary. That said, we're talking years ago. We've all grown up, and most of those people have moved away."

"That's why we should focus on the people in his inner circle now," Kieran said. "And his fans. I was looking through some of the comments on his latest book. It seems the reviews weren't as kind as those in the past."

"I'd noticed the same thing when I checked out a few sites last night," I said. "But if fans killed writers for bad books, there would be a lot more murders."

"Yes, from what his agent told me, though, he had received some rather disturbing emails and letters over the last year," Kieran said. "Some of the emails came with threats."

"Do you have access to those yet?"

"No," Sheila answered. "We're working with the provider in Dublin. Can't you hack them like you did the judge's?"

"Not without his laptop. Did you find it?"

Kieran cleared his throat. "Yes. It was at the cottage. Let's try to go through proper channels first. We have a few the agent forwarded on to us. I made some copies of those for you, as well."

So, James *did* have his laptop with him. Kieran handed me that pile of papers. It was odd that he was being so forthcoming. "Like I said, we've made copies of what we have so far for you."

I shook my head. "Why are you being so nice?"

He smirked. "As I said before, if we share information, perhaps you won't find yourself in dangerous situations where you almost die."

The last time that happened, I'd saved his life, but I wasn't going to remind him of that.

"Well, thanks. I'll take a look at all of this." My phone buzzed. I pulled it out. It was my alarm for an event at the library. "I'm headed to the library. But I'll let you know if I hear anything."

I got up to leave.

"Mercy?" he asked.

"Yes."

"Please, be careful. Leave the footwork to us. While I appreciate your help with the background on the case, there is no reason to put yourself in danger."

"I hear you, Detective Inspector."

Before heading to the library, I dumped the manuscripts on my desk at home, and then locked my office door. I wasn't hauling them around all day.

My phone buzzed. My editor Carrie's name came up.

"I'm going to make the deadline," I answered the question I knew was coming.

"Well, hello to you," she said. "But that isn't why I was calling. Did you murder James Brandt?"

I coughed. "What?"

"It's all over social media. Haven't you seen it? Can't say it has hurt your sales. In fact, numbers are up. But do I need to get you a good lawyer? And why are you always connected to dead people over there?"

"I was hoping, since this is such a small festival, no one would know we found the body."

"Oh, Mercy. When will you learn? Social media makes even the smallest place a hub for rumors."

"You can let everyone know at the publishing house that I didn't kill him. We did find the body, though. Why? What does it say on social media?"

"That you murdered him with a bookshelf. Quite clever, really. I never met the man, but I saw what he said to you online during the panels. I don't blame you, if you did kill him."

"Well, while I might have thought about killing him, it wasn't me."

"Why does this keep happening? You being the one to find dead bodies, that is? Again, not that it hurts your sales. It makes your fans even more curious about you. In fact, you made national news over here."

National news? Oh. My.

I sighed. "Just lucky, I guess. At least, this time the detective doesn't think I did it."

She laughed. "Is that *the* detective hottie?"

"Hottie? Have you been talking to Lizzie?"

"I'm guilty of texting her to see how the festival was going. She said you had the biggest turnouts. Good on you."

"You could just text me. Or were you asking her if I really was working on the book that I owe you in a month?"

"Oh, look at that. I have another call coming in. Love to you both. Stay out of jail. You need to finish your book." She hung up.

I was torn between wanting to laugh and feeling annoyed after Carrie's call. For me, social media was a necessary evil. It was how one sold books these days. I pulled up a couple of sites on my phone, and sure enough, an older picture of me was plastered all over the place with the headline: *Killer Writer?*

Great. This made it even more imperative I find the real murderer.

Before I left the house, I made sure everything was locked. One couldn't be too careful.

Then I headed out for a very busy day.

Later that night, I was at the store with Lizzie. We were cleaning up after the last signing of the day. Both of us were exhausted. I was the cliché introverted writer. Talking to fans and being in the public eye did not come naturally. It was something I'd learned to do through the years.

But it still wore me out mentally and physically. When I'd volunteered to do so many panels and readings to help the festival, I hadn't remembered what being out among the public did to my psyche. And meanwhile Lizzie had been rushed off her feet.

We were both very much ready for a long rest.

We were headed out the back door, and Lizzie called for Mr. Poe. But he refused to follow us; he sat in front of the cupboard that had a hidden door in the back. The door at the back of the cabinet opened into a storage area under the stairs.

"Come on, boy," she called. He was a very smart little dog, and Lizzie and I had fallen for him at first glance. He spent almost every day here with her.

He pawed the door and whined.

"He's been doing that all evening," she said. "Do you think we have mice?"

"I hope not. Maybe it wouldn't hurt to call an exterminator."

"I'm not a huge fan of vermin."

"I don't think most people are," I said.

I went to scoop up the tiny black dog, but he wiggled out of my arms and barked.

"Maybe I should check," I said.

She pushed past me and grabbed something out of her office.

"Here." She handed me a long umbrella with a pointy ferrule. "Just in case it is a mouse, and you have to shoo it away."

Oh great.

I opened the cupboard doors and stepped inside. When I pushed hard, the back panel opened. I reached around on the wall for the light. Then I stepped inside, but I had to squeeze through.

A foot blocked the door.

"Oh. My."

"Is it a rat? Don't let it run out."

"No. It isn't a rat. But I need you to call 999—again." I stepped carefully around the body on the floor. I knelt and then put my fingers on where there should have been a pulse. There wasn't one.

"Is that Sebrena?" Lizzie asked.

"It is," I replied.

And she was quite dead.

TEN

While the forensic team took over the bookstore, Kieran suggested Lizzie and I head home, but he made it clear that he would still need to speak to us. As we waited for him in our cottage, I made coffee while my sister baked a cherry pie. The recipe was our mother's, and we only ate it when things were not going our way.

Lizzie loved baking.

I had no idea how to even turn our oven on. Though, what I understood so far about the Aga was that it stayed on all the time and helped to heat our very cold kitchen.

I didn't usually drink coffee after two in the afternoon unless I was on deadline. But I needed my brain cells revived. I'd just found a very dead Sebrena in the bookstore and would soon have to speak to Kieran about it.

"How did she end up in our storeroom?" I asked. "We're the only ones who know about it, right?"

Lizzie shook her head. "It's not a secret. Caro knows about it. And I had volunteers in and out of there this whole week. It's where we kept most of the supplies for the signings and events. I don't have much room in the office, and it was just easier to use that space to store everything."

There was a knock on the front door. Lizzie leaned down to take the pie out of the oven, and I went to answer.

Kieran stood there, and his forehead was creased. I hadn't known him long but well enough that I understood he was worried.

"How did she die?" I asked.

"We'll have to wait for the postmortem, but there were no outward signs of trauma."

"Her lips were blue, though," I said. "Even in the dim light of the storeroom, I noticed that."

"Aye."

In the short time before the police had arrived, I'd taken a quick look around her and the scene. My investigation had been peripheral since I couldn't touch anything, other than when I'd searched for a pulse.

"Do you think it was poison?"

He sighed. "Like I said, no idea. And I will be the one asking the questions."

I bit my lip. "Right." I refused to apologize for my curiosity. It was innate and why I'd succeeded as a mystery writer.

"I made you some coffee."

A small smile lit his face. "I need it." He shared my love for coffee and my specialty machine that made the closest thing to a barista's version than any I'd ever tasted.

"Detective Inspector, let us know how we can help." Mercy was cleaning some dishes she used for the pie.

I handed him the cup of coffee I'd just poured.

He sniffed it and closed his eyes. "Cortado?"

"Of course." His favorite drink was something else we had in common.

"The pie will be ready soon," Mercy said as she sat down. "It's cooling."

I handed her a cup of chamomile tea she'd requested.

Mr. Poe sat by her chair. She scooped him up and held him against her chest. The strain of what had happened was evident in her eyes. She closed them and then breathed deeply.

The stress on her face pulled at my heartstrings. I would do anything to protect her from more pain. She'd been through far too much over the past year. But I couldn't put her in bubble wrap.

And we did have a bad habit of finding dead bodies.

"Let's start at the beginning," Kieran said to me. "How did you find the deceased?"

"Mr. Poe," I said.

Kieran raised his eyebrows. "What?"

"We were trying to leave the bookstore, but he refused. He kept pawing at the door to the hidden storage cupboard."

"He's a very smart boy," Lizzie said into his fur. He snuggled closer to her. While I loved that ball of fur, and he loved me, Lizzie was his person. "We thought it was mice."

Kieran appeared confused, but nodded.

"Mercy went to check, and that's when..." Her voice trailed off, and she closed her eyes. "I can't believe she's dead."

"When was the last time you each saw her?" he asked.

Lizzie took another deep breath.

"For me, it was yesterday during the signing for James," I said.

"How did that work?" he asked. "He's dead."

"Yes, but according to Sebrena, he'd signed thousands of bookplates. We used those."

"You said, *according*, like you didn't believe his agent."

Lizzie shot me a look.

"I thought she might have a few. Many of us sign bookplates for events and bloggers who are doing early reviews. But she said she had thousands that she gathered from James over the years."

"So, you think she forged them?"

"I'm saying it's a convenient possibility. She was quite aggressive when it came to sales and in continuing his legacy. You'll need an expert to check the handwriting. I may have borrowed one of the bookplates for analysis." I did finger quotes around borrowed.

"Mercy," Lizzie said with disbelief.

I shrugged. "I would have never made it public. I'd never do anything to hurt our store. I was just curious if she was telling the truth."

Kieran made a note in his book. "I'll need that for evidence."

"I'll get it for you." It was in my coat by the back door. I reached into the pocket and found it. Then I handed it over. He put it in an evidence bag he had in the pocket of his jacket and wrote on the outside.

"Did anything strange happen at the store during the signing?"

"Sebrena was behaving like she owned James's work," Lizzie said.

"She's right," I said. "The strangest thing was she held court like she'd written the book. We were just as confused as the fans. She even took selfies with them. You might want to look over the social media at the event for comments from the fans to gauge what they thought.

"It was honestly the weirdest book signing I've ever attended, and that is saying something."

He wrote more in his notebook.

"What was your take on her?" he asked me.

"You won't like me saying this, but Sebrena was my prime suspect right up until we found her dead."

He frowned. "Why is that?"

"They dated for a while, you know," I said. "You heard Sheila. James had a habit of dating women who were already in relationships." I hated saying that. It didn't make the women sound very strong or like they had a choice. "But then he ended it."

But I wasn't one to judge when it came to relationships. That area of my life had never been particularly successful. Made worse by the fact I'd been married to my career for most of my adult life.

"She didn't seem that upset by his death," Lizzie said. "Right after she found out, she threatened me if I sent any of his books back."

"Were the bookplates her idea?" he asked.

I pursed my lips. "Not exactly," I said. "I may have brought it up when I was trying to talk to her about James."

"So, you were being nosy and that was your way into the conversation?"

"You say nosy, I say curious. It was a way to help my sister move those books. But I still find it suspicious that she'd gathered thousands of bookplates over the years. Especially given that we had strict instructions that James would only sign for one hour."

He nodded. "Let's get back to when you last saw the victim."

"You said victim, so you do think she was killed. Why?"

He paused writing. "Like you noticed, the lips and eyes had a strange color."

I wasn't sure, as the storeroom had been fairly dark. And I'd tried not to disturb anything. But I had suspected it from the tinge of color around her lips.

"She came in a few times," Lizzie said. "To make sure we were ready for the events involving James's books. We'd sold out during the signing." She glanced at me.

"What?" It seemed like she'd remembered something.

"I told her I had a few more copies coming in a few days. As you know, the shipments had been delayed last week. She said she'd leave behind some bookplates for those. We'd been really busy, so I asked her to leave them in the storeroom, so they didn't get lost."

"So, she was in the storeroom today?" Kieran asked.

Lizzie rubbed her temples. "My days are running together. But yes, I saw her in the store this afternoon." Her eyes opened wide. "Oh."

"What?"

"There was a man. His back was to me. But I saw her arguing with someone this afternoon." She blinked. "Or was that yesterday? What is wrong with my brain?"

"It's the shock," Kieran said. His voice was gentle. I appreciated that he handled my sister with great kindness. She was still getting back on an even keel when it came to her emotions and nerves.

"Can you tell me anything about him?"

She blew out a breath. "I was in the back of the store, and they were near the front door. He had dark hair and wore a dark, long-sleeved T-shirt. But the sun was shining through the window, and they were in the glare. In fact, I don't remember seeing her after that."

"And you did see her go into the storeroom?"

"Well, like I said, that's where we'd been keeping supplies. I motioned to where it was at the back of the store and told her about the hidden cupboard door. I was busy at the front. I must admit I didn't see her go in there."

She cleared her throat.

"Do you think that's when she died? That was hours ago." A tear slid down her cheek. "If we'd known, maybe we could have saved her life. I should have checked."

I patted her hand. "Lizzie. Stop and breathe."

She did as I asked.

"You are in no way responsible for what happened," I said

gently. "You heard Kieran. She'd most likely been poisoned like James. Stop tying yourself into knots."

"I get that, but why didn't she call out?"

"Her death could have been instantaneous once the poison worked through her system," Kieran offered. He held up a hand. "I am in no way saying that is what happened. But it is a theory. It didn't appear the body had been dragged or moved. So, she most likely died on the spot. Had she appeared ill in any way?"

She shook her head. "She was kind of strange to begin with when it came to the way she acted regarding James's books. Maybe a tad neurotic. Everything had to be a certain way, and she was extremely picky. She was more demanding than all the other authors we've had combined. I hadn't noticed her being ill at all. But I'd also been busy. We had a line out the door for most of the day. The store has been bustling during the festival, for which I'm grateful."

"And you are certain you can't describe the man you saw her arguing with at your store any further?"

"No. I'm sorry. I only glanced up from the signing table for a few seconds. We had another author there, but Sebrena hadn't left yet. So, I was in the back of the first floor. They were by the front door and they were in a glare. The sun had come out for a few minutes. I just assumed she was talking to one of James's fans. But the argument looked heated."

"I see," he said. "Are there security cameras in the store?"

"I've never thought we needed them," she said. "My grandfather didn't see the need. Nor do I."

"We might want to look into them, though. Just for the future," I said.

She sighed. "I like the fact that we don't have to worry about crime here. But why do we keep finding dead bodies? It's terrible."

"Aye, it is," Kieran said.

"You don't suspect us, do you?" It was as if she'd just come to that realization, and her eyes went wide.

"No," he said. "But it is odd that you are the ones finding the bodies."

"Do you think someone is trying to set us up to take the blame?" I asked. That thought had just occurred to me.

"From what you said, they could not have known you would be the ones to show up at the cottage. In fact, my guess is they were trying to set up Sebrena. It was strange that she asked you two to go find him. I find her actions highly suspect. Except, now she's dead."

"So, you thought she killed him as well?"

"I don't make assumptions," he said. "However, the evidence was leaning in that direction. But now the lead suspect is dead. If it was poison, the killer may not have known how long it would take. It was most likely a coincidence she was in the storage room when she fell ill."

"We have the worst luck," Lizzie said. "I know that sounds callous. But, goodness, this is all so weird."

"I agree with you," I said.

"I need to make arrangements for the events for tomorrow," Lizzie said. "I assume you'll want me to keep the store closed."

"No. That's why forensics is in there tonight. They should have everything sorted by first thing tomorrow. I don't see why you can't open in the early afternoon."

"Really?" That was surprising. "Is it because she was poisoned and probably just passed out and died back there? That's why you don't think we did it? If we'd killed her, we would have tried to hide the body somewhere else. And we certainly wouldn't have called you."

"Mercy." My sister shook her head.

I waved a hand. "You know how my brain works," I said as an excuse. Sometimes, my thoughts came out of my mouth before I had a chance to stop them. I talked to myself while I worked. Who was I kidding? I talked to myself all the time. I always had characters in my head chatting. Talking out loud was how I stayed sane. Though, I wasn't always aware I was doing it.

"As a mystery writer, I hope you'd be cleverer." He smiled, and something happened in the pit of my stomach.

I ignored it.

My sister snorted and then giggled.

"Do you think we're looking at the same killer?" I asked. "I mean, I know you don't like to assume anything, but the deaths are similar."

"We will have to see what forensics and the evidence say," he said. "As you know, I do not believe in coincidence. Someone wanted both of them gone."

"We just have to figure out why, right?" I asked. "It always comes down to motive."

"Correct. But I would like to remind you that is my job. I'm bringing you in as a consultant only. You are not to put yourself or Lizzie's life in danger."

"What he said." Lizzie gave me the stink eye. "It's bad enough she died in our store. The last thing I need is for you to put us in the crosshairs of a killer again."

"Fine," I said. "I'll be careful." But it didn't really matter what they said. I would still look for answers. My mind wouldn't allow me to sit on the sidelines and wait for the detective to figure things out. I wasn't made that way.

After eating a piece of pie and finishing his coffee, the detective headed back to the crime scene.

"While the good detective inspector may not think we killed these people, that doesn't mean the rest of the town, and James's fans, won't," I said. "The sooner we find out who did and can clear our names, the better."

"Do you really think people blame us?" She sounded worried.

I shrugged. "We live in a small town, and as much as I'd like to say no, we're still outsiders. Plus, I looked at social media this afternoon for the festival. Many of his fans think it's odd we found his body. There are all kinds of conspiracy theories rolling around the internet."

She gave me a stricken look.

"No one thinks you had anything to do with it. The bookstore will be fine. I seem to be taking the brunt of the criticism online."

"I don't care about the bookstore. I'm worried about you. This could be terrible for your name and career."

I smiled. "Not according to Carrie. There are stories posted all over the internet that I killed James. It actually boosted my sales."

She shook her head. "People are weird."

"I don't disagree. I'm going to take a look at the older manuscript I told you about. There is no name on it, and I'm curious if it really is one of James's earlier works."

"Do you need help?" She was exhausted, I could tell by the look in her eyes.

"No. It's just a bit of reading."

She yawned. "Okay, I'm going to bed. We have another long day tomorrow."

I followed her to the stairs. She stopped and turned to me. And then she threw her arms around me. "I need a hug," she said.

I hugged her hard for more than a minute. "Don't worry," I said. "Everything is going to be okay."

"Someone is killing people and trying to make it look like we did it. So, it doesn't feel like things will be okay."

"Yes, but this time, the police don't think we murdered anyone. That's progress, right?"

She nodded.

"Get some sleep."

"Don't stay up too late. You have a writing workshop to teach first thing tomorrow at the library."

Darn. I'd forgotten that. Even though she'd put reminders in my phone and on my office calendar.

"I won't."

Mr. Poe followed her up the stairs. He slept at the end of her bed every night. Since the day he'd arrived in our lives, it was as if he had made it his mission to take care of Lizzie.

I loved that about the little dude.

I lit a fire in my office and settled down at my grandfather's large wooden desk. Lizzie once said the office had an Agatha Christie feel, and I didn't disagree. It was the opposite of my modern office in New York, but I'd written many words already in this space, and I wasn't about to change it.

I pulled the copy of the older manuscript out of the desk drawer where I'd locked it away. One couldn't be too safe when protecting evidence. I'd learned that the hard way. Several months ago, I'd hidden a file folder with information about our grandfather in a cabinet under our bathroom sink, and a murderer had stolen it. The police believed she must have burned it. Whatever had been in that file was gone forever.

I'd been furious because the information had been about our grandfather. My sister and I were desperate to know more about him and our father. Every morsel of information helped us understand them better.

The manuscript did not have a title page. It just started with chapter one. The writing was definitely by a newbie. The point of view hopped around, and the novel rambled at the beginning with way too much backstory and description.

The missing girl didn't show up until the end of chapter three. But that was when things became interesting.

ELEVEN

The next morning at the library, I'd come to the end of my beginner's writing class and opened the floor up for questions. Time had gone by quickly, but I was looking forward to a cup of coffee. I'd stayed up way too late reading the older manuscript. It left me with even more questions about why James had it on his table at the cottage.

Hands went up.

Focus.

I took a few questions, all of which were writing-related. The class was packed, and I was surprised no one asked about James's death, given the rumors that had come out of the festival.

The biggest surprise was that several of our neighbors from the court were there. When the class was over, Rob and Scott, followed by Brenna, whose home was on the other side of us, walked to the front where I stood.

"That was amazing," Rob said. "I've written cookbooks, but writing fiction is so different."

"I'm grateful you helped fill seats, but what are you all doing here?"

"We wanted to support you and find out if you and Lizzie are okay," Brenna said. She looked like a supermodel, even in her jeans, furry sweater, and boots.

I smiled.

"They're being nosy," Scott said. "I came because I've always wanted to write a book."

Rob gave him a look of incredulity.

"It's true, so it is," Scott said. "Not a mystery, mind you. I want to write a sci-fi and fantasy novel along the lines of *Star Wars*, or maybe *Dune*."

I wasn't surprised since I'd seen his collection of books at his house. "You should," I said encouragingly.

Several people stood behind them, waiting to chat with me. A few of them held books they probably wanted me to sign. "How about we meet at the pub for lunch? I'll fill you in there."

"We were thinking we'd meet at ours," Rob said. "More privacy there. I'll make you pork tacos. We've already asked Lizzie, and she said yes."

I laughed. "Sounds good. And like you've planned it all. When?"

"We checked. You have a break at noon."

"Okay, I'll see you then."

The three of them and Lolly had become great friends and the best neighbors I'd ever had. I was surprised they'd waited this long to find out what was going on. Also, their festival duties took them to different places, and it wouldn't hurt for them to keep an eye out for anything strange.

After answering a few more questions and signing some books, I headed out of the library. Kieran waited outside for me. He appeared worried.

"What's wrong?" I asked.

There were several people eyeing us curiously.

"Come with me to the station," he said, glancing around.

"I'm not in trouble, am I?"

He cocked his head. "Why? What did you do now?"

We both laughed.

"No," he said. "I have news that I don't plan on sharing with the rest of the world. There are too many people around here."

He wasn't wrong. I followed him to the station and then to his office.

"The toxicology came back," he said. "They were killed with the same poison. And it was in the tea." He sat down behind his desk.

"So, what was it?"

He stared down at his desk.

"You don't want to tell me, do you?"

"Goes against all of my training," he said.

I sat down across from him. "Right. Never share information during an ongoing investigation. But what if we did a quid pro quo? Besides, you promised not to get hung up on procedures. You know I can help."

"You first," he said.

I glanced down at my phone. I had about twenty minutes before I had to be at the bookstore, which was a half-block down.

"I read through the older manuscript last night."

"And was it his?"

"That I can't tell you. It was very beginner-ish, and most likely written by someone young. But the story, well, that was interesting."

"Tell me," he encouraged.

"It was about a missing teen, and it takes place in Dublin. The thing is, I need to do more research, but it's about a group of friends from a small town who go to Dublin for the weekend. Five of them go, and only four return."

He frowned and rubbed his head. "I don't remember anything like that happening here."

"I think possibly because most of the investigation took

place in Dublin. But I did some research last night. A Keeley
Boyle went missing in Dublin in 1995. She was there with
friends – James, the mayor, Mark Patrickson, and Finneas
Hughes – celebrating her birthday, and went missing from a
pub. She'd be in her fifties now."

"The same age as James," he said softly.

"I only had access to a few articles, but he was there. The
newspaper reports said foul play was suspected, but nothing
was proven."

"I'm not sure I like where this is going, especially if it
involves the mayor."

"Right. But the writer intimates one of them murdered her,
and the others helped dispose of the body. The police came to
the conclusion she'd run off and started a new life.

"The thing is, one of the friends from school went on to be a
botanist. His name in the article was Finneas Hughes."

"Doctor Hughes the botanist? He lives out on the cliff."

"Yes, and later this afternoon he'll be teaching a class on
using poisons in mysteries and thrillers."

Kieran's brows furrowed. "Let me guess, you plan on
attending."

"Well, yeah. But are you going to pull him in?"

He shook his head. "Not yet. Unlike you, I need physical
evidence to tie him to the murders. If he is guilty, we can't show
our cards until we have a better reason to hold him. He's also a
good friend of the mayor, so I have to go by the book."

"The tea was poisoned, isn't that enough?"

"No prints. Anyone could have made the tea. But the
poison was one everyone in Ireland knows about, it's called
lords-and-ladies, and also cuckoo-pint. I can't remember the
science term. You don't touch it. We learn that from an early
age."

"I've never heard of it. Trust me, I've done a lot of research
in that regard." I didn't mean to sound like a know-it-all, but I

used poisons a great deal in my work, and I never stopped learning about them.

"Like I said, I need prints or DNA to link him to the crimes. Or, at the very least, eyewitness accounts of him being at the cottage."

"Pesky evidence," I said.

He laughed, but it wasn't a happy sound. "Who else was mentioned in the articles you read, and can you forward those to me?"

"A teen named Mark Patrickson. I couldn't find much about him."

His eyebrows went up.

"What is it?"

"Mark Patrickson is Chef Patrick. That is what he goes by now. And my guess is he was a part of that same group. He's about the same age."

I'm sure my eyes were the size of saucers. "As in the guy who is catering all of our literary events and handling the food?"

"One and the same," he said as he shuffled through some papers.

My phone alarm went off. "I've a few things to do, but I'll attend the professor's class later today. I'd planned on doing so anyway."

"He's a bit of a hermit," he said. "I'm surprised they got him to speak at the festival."

"He has a new book coming out—an academic one," I said. I'd checked the schedule when I thought the name sounded familiar. "Probably his publisher didn't give him a choice about doing publicity. That happens, even in the world of academia."

"I may sneak into the event as well."

"Oh, we're meeting at Rob's for lunch. Would you like to join the court gang?"

"They're just going to pry for information."

I nodded. "I'll only tell them 'bits and bobs', as you like to say. They are helping out all over the festival. We could use them to keep an eye on our suspects. You're understaffed with the events for the festival."

He shook his head. "Do not mention the mayor or the botanist—actually, no names or type of poison. We can't risk someone learning that information. It's something we're keeping quiet about."

"I'm going to have to tell them something. You've met them."

He grunted. "I can't keep you from telling them about your experience in finding the bodies. But anything I've shared with you must be kept quiet. Or I won't be sharing any more."

"Noted."

His phone rang. "I've got to take this. Let me know if you hear or see anything. And be safe."

"Always."

He huffed before answering his phone and I decided to see myself out.

After another author's reading, Lizzie and I escaped for lunch. Scott and Rob's beautiful garden assailed the senses with roses and other flowery delights. The one good thing about the rain in Ireland was the lush landscapes it created.

When Scott opened the front door, the warm, spicy smells from the kitchen wafted through the house.

"Oh. My. That smells like Texas," Lizzie said.

We laughed.

"He's been cooking like a demon," Scott said. "We have enough for a small army. You've met him. He never does anything small."

Rob was a talented chef, and also the sweetest man.

We headed toward the kitchen, but Scott paused in front of the dining room, where Lolly and Brenna sat at a beautifully decorated table. Spring flowers were in low, crystal vases on a sapphire tablecloth.

"This is beautiful," Lizzie said. "If you came to ours for lunch, we'd be at the kitchen table with our daily-use plates and cutlery."

"Same," Brenna said. "But it's Rob."

"He was taking pictures earlier with a fancy camera," Lolly said. "I came early to see if I could help. I think he'll be using this in one of his cookbooks."

Scott pulled out chairs for us. "The literary festival has inspired him to work even faster on his new cookbook."

"I'm traveling around the world with this one," Rob said as he came in with giant platters filled with spiced pork and corn tortillas.

"Did you hand-make the tortillas?" Lizzie asked.

"Of course," he said. "I had to order some special masa, but I promise these are worth it."

He sat the platters down in the middle of the table. "There's more. Hon, come help me," he said to Scott.

His partner followed him to the kitchen. A minute later, they brought in rice and beans.

"I'm going to need a nap after this one," I said.

They all laughed.

"I'm curious how the festival is going, compared to past years," Lizzie said as we passed the platters around the table.

"Attendance is up by a few thousand, and I think we have your sister to thank for that," Lolly said.

"Me?"

"Yes, dear," Lolly said. "You're the biggest author we've ever had at our little festival."

"On this side of the pond, I thought that would have been James," I said honestly.

"I'm sure his presence didn't hurt, but you're the one most

of the new visitors came to see," Lolly said. "We have been checking the comment cards."

"I'm glad I could help." I was certain my cheeks were pink from embarrassment. I was aware that my novels had hit a certain level when it came to sales, but I would never grow used to the celebrity that came with that.

I was still just me. And no one was more surprised than me that my books were appreciated by so many.

"I've never thought about writing a book until today," Brenna said. "Maybe a photography book, so a lot less writing. But you really inspired me to tell stories my way." She was a talented photographer and did commercial, trade, and fashion shoots.

"You should," Lizzie said. "I'd buy that book and carry it in the store. Your photos are amazing."

My sister wasn't wrong. "Would you do fashion or more of your travels?"

Brenna traveled all over the world for her work and always took extra time to photograph the world around her.

"Probably travel," she said. "That way I wouldn't have to get permission from the models and designers. That would be a real headache."

"I can imagine," I said.

"Your travel photos are gorgeous," Lizzie said. "You always make me want to go to the places you shoot."

"I was just thinking the same thing," I said.

"You are both sweet. Maybe I really will do a book."

"You should," I said. "And while I know very little about photography, I'll help you however I can."

"I may take you up on that," she said.

I ate some pork taco, and the spicy meat tingled along my tongue with just the right amount of heat. "Yum," I said. "We won't ever miss Texas with you cooking for us, Rob."

He grinned. "Thank you. I'm glad to do whatever we can to keep you here."

"Oh, we aren't going anywhere," Lizzie said.

Our friends all glanced at one another.

What was that about?

"I'm happy to hear you say that," Lolly said. "That is, given the latest trouble."

The murders were bound to come up.

"Are the rumors about us awful?" Lizzie asked. "Mercy said there was a lot of stuff online. I've been afraid to look."

"I do not know about online, but no one in town believes you had anything to do with those poor souls," Lolly said. "It is unfortunate you were the ones to find them both. I cannot imagine how awful that was for you. I've been worried it is too much, and you might want to run back to America."

Lizzie shook her head. "I don't understand why this keeps happening to us. But we aren't going anywhere. I love Shamrock Cove and you all."

Brenna patted her hand. "We feel the same way about you and Mercy. And I hate to be nosy, but can you tell us anything? Other than finding them dead had to be terrible?"

"We promised Kieran that we wouldn't say anything," I said. "And you've read most of what happened in the papers already. But I do have some questions for you all."

They'd lived here far longer than my sister and I, and I hoped they had some answers.

TWELVE

"I had a feeling you'd say you couldn't tell us anything," Rob said across the table. "But why would you have questions for us? We didn't know either of the poor people who died."

"Lolly, did," I said. "I was doing some research last night, and I wondered if you might remember a case where a young woman went missing in 1995?" I turned to Lolly. "She went to Dublin with a group of friends – James, the mayor, the chef catering our events, oh and Professor Finneas Hughes – but never returned to Shamrock Cove." I found it odd that two of those men were on my suspect list.

Lolly frowned. "Aye, the young woman was Keeley Boyle. Her family moved away years ago. The story isn't what you may have read about it, though."

"Oh? Do you remember why they didn't suspect the friends?"

"It was kept quiet, but they found her not long after she went missing," Lolly said.

"They found her alive?" Lizzie asked before I could. I hadn't told her anything that I'd discovered. That was her natural curiosity bubbling to the surface. She liked to say I was the only one with a nose for trouble, but she was just as bad.

"Aye. She ran off to America with her boyfriend. If I remember correctly, he's her husband now. Her home life with her da, who liked his drink, wasn't very pleasant. The friends helped her to run away. Since she was an adult, there wasn't much the family could do. As far as I know, she's still living in America somewhere."

"Oh," I said confused. That was not at all how the mystery I'd read had gone. I'd been so focused.

"What's wrong?" Scott asked.

I told them about the book. I didn't think that would be sharing too much information since it was obviously a work of fiction and not based on the facts of the case.

"Do you think James wrote it?" Lolly asked.

I shrugged. "The writing is so different. I don't know."

"Hmmm. Years ago, I remember some original manuscripts by Irish writers going missing from the library," Lolly said. "If I remember, the same group of friends was implicated in the theft. They were in secondary school back then, and nothing was ever proven."

"But this wasn't anything special—not that I like to say that about anyone's writing. I just can't see why someone would bother stealing it. There was no name on this manuscript, and it was missing a title page. I'd think if it were one that was kept in the library, it might be more identifiable or stamped in some way. The one I read only had page numbers and nothing that identified the author or title of the work. What I don't understand is whether it was one that was taken years ago or an early one of James's. And why did he have it out with his own manuscript?"

Or was there something in there that he didn't want others to know? I needed to read through it again. When I read it the first time, I thought I'd be looking for clues about a missing woman. But apparently Keeley had been found safe.

When investigating, going in with preconceptions was never a good thing. I needed to look at the manuscript objectively.

"Lolly, is there anything you know about James and his family that might help the police with their investigation? I mean, I'm sure your grandson has asked. I'm just curious," I said.

She shook her head. "They kept themselves to themselves," she said. "The whole family was not overly friendly. At least, as far as I can remember. They moved away when he was in university. His ma was in the garden club. Grew a lovely chrysanthemum that one, but was always prickly, like my summer roses."

I smiled. Gardens were everything to Lolly. Her back and front yards were beautiful oases on the court. Well, everyone on the court had beautiful gardens. It was a rule that they had to be kept up. Luckily, my sister had a green thumb.

"Speaking of flowers, what do you know about Doctor Finneas Hughes?"

Lolly laughed. "When he was a young one, he was quite the troublemaker. None of us ever believed he'd amount to anything. Now, he's a professor and a scientist. He's been a recluse since he left the university."

"He seems young to have retired."

Lolly nodded. "He left to take care of his wife. Brought her here to the seaside for her health. Bless her, she passed a few years ago. He never went back to teaching. Though, from what I understand, he still does research and writes books. He's a highly regarded botanist, not just here but across Ireland. He's won several accolades for his discoveries.

"We very seldom see him in town, though. He has an assistant, housekeeper, and butler who handle anything he might need. I've only seen him once or twice in the pub since his wife died. I was surprised when he agreed to speak at our event. We've been reaching out for years."

I, too, wondered why he did. Though I had a feeling it had to do with his publishers. While those in the world of academia didn't have the same sort of success quotient as other writers, they were still expected to participate in signings and such when the opportunities arose.

"Is it just me, or does this group of friends seem to have more trouble than most?" Scott asked. "I mean, one is murdered. Another had to run away from a bad family. The third's wife died tragically."

"Who else was in their friend group?" Rob asked.

"The mayor, Thomas Gilfoy," I said.

"And there is Patrick, who is our caterer this weekend," Lolly said.

"Next year, it will be me," Rob said.

Lolly nodded. "Yes, it will. You should have put a bid in earlier."

Rob nudged Scott. "I had to convince this one that it was a temporary gig and that I wouldn't get stressed out."

Before they'd moved to Shamrock Cove, Rob had a couple of successful brick-and-mortar restaurants. He'd had a break-down from the stress and scared his partner to death. Scott was extremely protective of the talented chef and insisted he keep his workload manageable.

"Part of that promise is that you will hire a complete team to help out, and you won't try to do it all on your own," Scott said.

These two loved each other so much it gave me hope that relationships could work.

That was something I'd never been successful at when it came to dating and men. My sister said I had a homing device for narcissistic jerks. She never understood how someone as smart as me could end up with men like that.

In all honesty, I was equally perplexed. So much so, that I'd given up on dating several years ago to focus solely on my career. Back home, I'd go out with friends or meet in fun places with my various writer buds, but I didn't date.

"Oh, is it true that Chef Patrick used to be married to the woman who died, Sebrena?" Rob asked. "I read that on one of the gossip sites. I may have been looking up dirt on him. I don't necessarily like his food."

"It has been sort of bland," my sister said. Then she slapped her hand over her mouth. "I can't believe I said that out loud."

We laughed.

"It's just after tasting your food, there is no comparison," she said.

"Well, part of that is he's cooking for a large Irish crowd," Lolly said. "We did ask that he make the food palatable for many people with special dietary needs."

"Doesn't mean it has to be flavorless," Rob said. He gave us a mischievous smile. "There are ways to get flavor in without adding heat."

"Well, we will be lucky to have you next year," Lolly said. "But to answer your question. Yes, he was a part of that small group of friends. From what I remember, yes, he was married to her."

"And James stole Patrick's wife, who then became James's agent," Lizzie said. "Unfortunately, from what my sister has learned, Patrick had some sort of alibi for her demise."

I'm surprised my jaw didn't hit the floor in shock. "Have you been reading my notes?"

She shrugged. "When you pass out at your desk and leave your notebook open, I may have trouble not looking at what you've written."

Everyone laughed.

"Do you know why Sebrena was at your store when she died?" Scott asked.

Lizzie shook her head. "She'd been there earlier in the day, but no. There's no telling when we would have found her if it hadn't been for Mr. Poe." She glanced at her watch. "He's due his walk. I left him at the store with Caro since he was asleep. I should get going."

We thanked Rob for the food and took our leave.

"Where are you headed next?"

"I'm going to Doctor Hughes's class on poisons," I said.

She gave me the eye.

"What?"

"Just be careful. What if he's the one killing people?"

"I'm just going to learn about poisons. A mystery writer can never know too much."

"Promise me you'll be careful," she said with an exasperated sigh.

I put my hand on my heart. "I won't get myself murdered."

"I wish you'd take this seriously," she said. "You know how dangerous it can be if you poke the bear."

"Okay, no poking the bear or perhaps, in this case, the botanist."

But I did have some questions for the bear, and I was going to ask them.

I wasn't sure if it was the professor's monotone voice or if I'd eaten one too many pork tacos, but I had a tough time keeping my eyes open during his lecture.

The slightly balding man wore a tweed jacket and a plaid shirt. None of which went together. I found him to be a cliché of the absent-minded professor. He'd pause briefly and shuffle through his mess of papers on the podium before continuing with his lecture.

Most of the poisons he covered were ones I already knew about. My mind wandered, while I waited to ask my question about the poison that Kieran had mentioned earlier.

"Now, Agatha Christie was quite fond of..."

At the mention of Christie, I tuned back in, but wasn't surprised when he mentioned she was a big fan of cyanide.

"Doctor Hughes, we are nearing the end of your time. We need to take some questions," the moderator for his class cut in during the last ten minutes.

He frowned, but then nodded. "Right. Questions?" He said the words as if they were a challenge. No one raised their hand except for me.

His eyebrows went up. "Yes?" he said brusquely.

"I was curious about a specific poison and where it might be grown," I said.

"And that is?" he asked with no patience.

"I've been researching plants found in Ireland, and I was curious about cuckoo-pint."

He jerked his head back as if I'd slapped him.

Why did he react like that?

"What do you want to know?"

"I guess how it works," I said. "As a writer, I'm always looking for new ways to kill people." I tried to make a joke of it.

Several of those in the crowd laughed.

"The toxicity of arum maculatum is quite high," he said. "It is sometimes called lords-and-ladies, as well. The plant should be handled only by professionals, and is extremely dangerous to animals and humans. It is, however, not toxic to the birds who eat the berries and propagate the seeds. It is an invasive plant but only found in a few places in Ireland. One of which is the cliffs of Shamrock Cove."

It grew here. That was interesting. "So, it's rare?"

"That's what I said. The roots, and tuber, were sometimes used as a starch for linens, but that is no longer true. There have been a few initiatives to eradicate it, as it is so dangerous. It can sometimes be found in hedgerows but should be left alone."

"Would it be possible to hide the taste in food or drink?" I asked. I smiled, as if I were only asking for a book.

"The roots can be harvested – again, as a starch. The berries, which are quite poisonous, have an acrid taste. And would most likely make the mouth tingle if they were consumed."

"Other questions?" he asked. Looking around the room.

No one put their hand up. So, of course, I did.

He wasn't happy about it, but he nodded toward me. "Right? One more?"

"Would something like peppermint tea hide the taste?"

He frowned. "If it were heavily sugared, perhaps. I cannot say that I've ever tried it, as I'm standing before you today."

"Thanks," I said.

After the class was over, I had a break. I tried to find Dr. Hughes, but he disappeared. As in by the time I made my way through the crowd to the front of the room, he was gone.

I hurried outside but didn't see him.

Darn.

I did see Chef Patrick, though. He wore his chef coat and was hurrying toward the big banquet hall at the church. This evening's event was black tie, and more awards would be given to writers who hadn't been published yet. I'd been on the committee to help judge the entries and had been surprised by how good they were.

I didn't have anything to do until it was time to get ready, so I followed the chef. But when I arrived in the banquet hall, I only found those who were setting things up.

Scott and Rob were there putting out tablecloths and centerpieces.

"Hey, Mercy," Rob said. "You're early for the events."

"I was looking for Chef Patrick. I thought I saw him come in this way."

They shook their heads.

"He didn't come in here," Scott said. "Maybe he's in the kitchen?"

"Thanks, gang. Carry on with your magic. You're doing a beautiful job."

I was headed to the kitchen when a man stepped out of one of the side rooms, and I smacked into the back of him.

"Ooof, sorry."

"Are you okay?" He reached out to steady me. It was Chef Patrick. He was the epitome of tall, dark, and handsome. His black hair dipped down, almost covering one eye. He was unusually tan, as if he spent as much time outdoors as he did in the kitchen.

His bright blue eyes were laser focused on me.

I blinked, trying to remember why I had been chasing him.

"Yes, thank you for keeping me from doing a face-plant." He had a pound of flour in his other hand and smiled down at me. He really was quite good-looking.

"It is not a problem. You're the famous writer, Mercy something. I've seen you at some of the events. I'm sorry, I'm not much of a reader."

"I won't hold it against you," I said, sticking out my hand. "I'm Mercy McCarthy. It's nice to meet you. I must say, I'm surprised that you're still working."

He frowned. "Why wouldn't I be?"

"You were married to Sebrena, right? Terrible what happened. My sister and I were the ones who found her," I said quickly.

"That must have been awful for you," he said it as if he genuinely meant it.

"It was. I'm sorry for your loss."

"Aye. I'm still processing," he said. "That's the reason I'm working. We weren't close anymore. I had not seen her in years, but 'tis strange that she's no longer in the world."

"That must be so tough. Someone you once loved being murdered like that."

"So, it was murder?" He seemed shocked.

Darn it, Mercy. Kieran would kill me if he found out I'd said something to a suspect. It was something in the chef's eyes like I wanted to tell him everything about myself.

I shrugged. "I know probably about as much as you do. I just assumed foul play since Sebrena and James died within a day of one another." I hoped that was a good enough cover. I really had to get better about keeping my mouth shut.

"Do the police still think it was one of James's fans who was upset?" he asked. "I've been reading reports online that have been saying it might be. I believe you were mentioned in a few of the articles."

Ugh. Was everyone on social media?

"I can assure you—it wasn't me. I didn't know either of them well enough to want them dead. Why do you ask about a fan?"

"Well, first it was you who supposedly killed them, right? But I don't think anyone really believes that. Like I said, some of the rumors I read online were that it was a crazed fan. It's scary to think there are people like that running around in the world."

"It must be so difficult to lose someone you were married to, though. I can't even imagine what that must be like for you."

"Sebrena was—one of a kind, you might say. We'd made our amends. So, yes. It is tough. I will help the police in any way I can to find her killer. She didn't deserve to die like that."

"Were you still married when she went off with James?"

Great segue, Mercy. I did an internal sigh. I had a lot to learn when it came to questioning suspects.

His smile dissipated, and his eyes narrowed.

"I didn't realize it at the time, but he did me a great favor by taking her off my hands. Like I said, it was long ago, and we had made our amends."

Was that true? His former wife seemed more the type to rub things in his face rather than make amends. But again, that was just an assumption. I had no way to prove he wasn't telling me the truth.

"Now, if you will excuse me. We're running behind in the kitchen."

"I—uh." But before I could ask him a question, he took off.

He didn't seem like a killer. And how would he know about the cuckoo-pint? From what the botanist had said, handling the flowering plant at all could be quite dangerous. The poison had been mixed in the tea, which meant someone would have had knowledge of the dangers. Or they themselves might end up dead.

Could it have been Sebrena and she accidentally killed herself? But I just couldn't see the picky woman traipsing around the countryside, carefully collecting plants to kill her most profitable client.

I was no closer to an answer.

It had to be someone who knew how to handle the poison. The meek Dr. Hughes popped into my brain. He seemed the one person who would know how to handle the plant that killed our victims.

But why would he kill James and Sebrena?

This case was so confusing. I hoped Kieran had better luck than I did.

Solving cases was much easier when one made up the motive, facts, and clues.

THIRTEEN

That night at the New Writers' banquet, I had difficulty eating the stuffed chicken on my plate. Even though I didn't think Chef Patrick killed our victims, I just couldn't seem to put anything he'd made into my mouth.

"Are you nervous?" Lizzie asked softly. She sat next to me at our table near the front. Luckily, our neighbors were our guests. So, I didn't feel like I had to be on form all the time. That didn't keep the occasional fan from coming up and asking me to sign books, which I didn't mind. But it was nice to just hang out with our friends.

"I'm not hungry," I said.

She gave me a look. I never had trouble eating, and I was certain she was suspicious. But my fears about the food seemed silly and I didn't want to share.

James was supposed to be the master of ceremonies this evening, but with him gone it was up to me to get us all through the awards program. While the awards at the last gala dinner had gone to published authors, tonight's awards were for unpublished writers. I'd helped judge many of the manuscripts.

Rob escorted Lolly to the podium at the front of the room.

"Almost time," Lizzie said beside me.

I had a script written for the program, and I jotted down a few bullet points for my part.

"Hello, I'm Lolly O'Malley, Chairperson of our Shamrock Cove Literary Festival." There was a great deal of applause. "Before we begin our festivities, I would like to thank our mistress of ceremonies, Mercy McCarthy, for taking over tonight."

There was more applause.

"While our hearts go out to James Brandt's family, friends, and fans, we are grateful Mercy could step in at the last minute. Good luck to all of the nominees. I can tell you the competition was stiff this year, and our panel of judges would be the first to tell you that the competition truly was fierce. Now, please welcome mystery author, Mercy McCarthy."

People stood and applauded. As I moved behind the podium, I waved them down.

"Thank you, Lolly. As she said, the competition was a great one this year. Every nominee should be proud of the fact that they made it as a finalist in their category. There was a time, dear writers, when I sat exactly where you are tonight. Nerves took over, and my hands shook while I waited for them to announce the category my entry was in. I won't keep you waiting tonight. Good luck to you all."

One after another, I asked my fellow judges to announce the winners of each genre.

At the very end, it was my job to give the award for best book overall.

I opened the envelope and announced the winner. A man who was incredibly young, as in university age, came up. The smile on his face charmed my heart. I'd read his entry and imagined him to be much older. He was an incredibly gifted writer for one so young.

"Congratulations," I said as I handed him the award. "Would you like to say something?"

"Aye, that would be grand," he said.

I stepped out of the way.

"We love you," someone screamed out. The crowd laughed, as did the young writer.

"That would be me mam. Thank you, Mam, for putting up with me. She and Da are quite supportive of my writing. I'm lucky to have people who believe in me. Mam forced me to enter the contest. I'll admit I was afraid. So, thank you to the judges. I'm as happy as I've ever been." He stepped away from the podium and held up his award.

"How lucky are we to have such wonderful authors who are up and coming in our literary world?" I asked.

The audience clapped.

"I want to congratulate all of our winners, but also, again, for everyone who entered. There are several days left of our wonderful festival. Go to as many readings, signings, and classes as you can. Soak it all up. And I'll see you around."

The audience stood and clapped. They were being kind. I hadn't said anything that warranted it.

We were all leaving when I noticed Chef Patrick out by his van. He was arguing with someone, but I couldn't see who it was. He pointed a finger and shook his head.

But by the time the crowd of people cleared, the catering van had gone.

"Did you see who Chef Patrick was arguing with?" I asked Lizzie.

"No." She glanced over my shoulder. "Was he?"

I sighed. "Yes."

"Do you think he killed his ex?"

I shrugged. "I don't know. He had more of a reason than most. But he seemed genuinely sorry about her death when I spoke to him earlier. This case is so confusing."

"It is, which is why you should leave the investigation to the police. Two people have died, Mercy. You have to be careful. What if he is the killer, and now he's on to you?"

"No. It wasn't like that. I literally ran into him outside the church kitchen. I gave him no reason to suspect me of anything."

"Still."

I waved a hand. "I know. I know."

Tomorrow morning, I'd go to the station to see if Kieran was any closer to finding the killer.

I certainly wasn't. We were headed down the block when Lizzie stopped and turned around.

I glanced back to see what she was doing. "What's wrong?"

She shivered. "I have that feeling someone is watching us," she whispered.

I peered around her shoulder. "I don't see anyone," I whispered back. "But I trust that feeling." After living in Manhattan for years and dealing with stalkers, I'd learned to trust my own internal alarms. I had a stalker there who had put me on edge. And every time I had the feeling someone watched me here in Ireland, I feared that person had crossed the pond.

I'd hoped to get away from all of that living here, but maybe it was just the paranoia that had followed me to Shamrock Cove.

And one thing I hadn't thought about was the fact that we'd been all over the news sites online. My stalker could have found out where we were. This time I was the one who shivered.

Lizzie hooked her arm in mine, and we hurried to the secret door that led into the court where we lived. Once inside our house's foyer, we took a deep breath.

Mr. Poe ran up to great us. Lizzie scooped him up in her arms and held him close. We often took him everywhere with us, but he'd still been eating his dinner when we had to leave.

He was an easy-going pup, except when it came time for his meals. In that respect, he was quite demanding.

As she squeezed him to her chest, her hands shook.

"Are you okay?"

She nodded. "I'm tired. That's all. It's been a good week at the store, but so busy. And..."

"It's stressful that we're in the middle of another murder investigation."

Her eyes went wide. "Yes. It's not your fault or mine, but here we are. I thought we would be safe in Shamrock Cove. I don't like thinking there is danger around every corner."

"It's temporary," I said. "Try to remember that."

She nodded. "I'm going to let Mr. Poe out and then I'm headed to bed."

"Okay, sleep well."

I was restless and went to my grandfather's library. It was one of my favorite rooms in the house. He had his personal collection of first editions and favorite books. Several weeks ago, I'd done a quick assessment of just one shelf of his collection, and it was worth well over three hundred thousand dollars. Lizzie and I had finally figured out that these books were the treasure he'd mentioned in the will where he'd left us everything.

He'd also left us clues about a mystery involving our father, which we were still researching. I'd reached out by letter to the Irish and British governments as to whether they had any information about our father, who went missing in action.

So far, we'd heard nothing back. We had found letters saved in various books from our grandmother to our grandfather, as well as some letters our grandfather had been sent during the war from our father to our mother. Letters she'd never received or knew about when she was alive.

We hadn't known about our grandfather until his lawyer

reached out to us after his death. From all accounts, he'd been a good man who had found out about us at the end of his life. He'd left us with several mysteries, including what happened to our father.

Our mother had never talked about our father much. She called him the donor, so we'd never known anything about him. Our father's relationship with our grandfather—at least as far as we'd read in letters we found—had been an uneasy one.

Once every few weeks, we'd search the house and the bookstore to find more clues or letters. As for the treasure mentioned in the will, we'd decided a few weeks ago he'd been talking about his books. But it didn't keep us from looking for more clues.

That and he had wondered in one of his letters if our father was still alive. That didn't seem likely, but we continued our search.

I loved the feel of the library. From the scent of old leather to the soft cushy chairs, I found myself in here more and more often. Sometimes, I worked on my laptop. Other times, it was just to read. I'd grabbed the old manuscript that had been found at James's house and sat down.

Now that I understood it was most likely a work of fiction rather than clues to the current murders, I hoped to look at it from a different point of view. I skimmed the pages, but nothing jumped out at me.

And I still had no idea if it was one of James's early books. The writing was so different.

I did pick up on the strained relationships with friends in the book. They blamed each other for the girl vanishing. In the end, they'd all gone their separate ways.

And in the book, the missing woman was believed to be murdered. According to the novel, it had been her boyfriend at the time who had committed the heinous crime.

But the real Keeley Boyle had survived her ordeal. And the friends had known that.

Since writers often took real-life situations and reworked them for fiction, I tried to look at the situation more objectively. If it hadn't been Keely who died, had there been someone else? Was this some kind of giant cover-up?

Maybe he'd thought about revising it and using the story in a new way.

I set the book down on the side table by the cushy chair where I'd curled up. I stretched and took a deep breath.

I should have used my nervous energy to write, but my mind was too scattered. Sometimes, when I had trouble writing, getting away from it was the answer. I wasn't sleepy, so I went around the room in search of some new books to look through.

Using the library ladder, I decided to be more methodical. I started with the top shelf of the north wall. The books up here were dustier, and I wiped them down with a cotton rag as I put them back. When I'd finished the top shelf, I moved my way down to the next one.

The second book in, my breath caught. The inside of the book had been hollowed out. Well, it had been designed that way. But the letters were from my grandfather to our grandmother. After reading the first letter, which left my eyes watery, I decided to save the rest for Lizzie and me to go through together. There had been a great love between our grandparents, which made me think of Lizzie and her fiancé.

I pushed the ladder back to the corner of the room and took the book full of letters to my office.

There was a letter unopened in the pile. I wondered if my grandfather had missed it. Usually, I would wait for Lizzie to open it, but I was curious as to why it was unopened. There was no return address.

I carefully used the letter opener. And pulled the weathered paper out. I pursed my lips as I read:

Dear Father,

I have regrets about our last conversation. I do not know if you have received my other letters, as I'm on a mission, and we cannot receive mail. I understand why you did not want me to join the military, but this was something I had to do.

I cannot tell you where I am or why, but please know that I love you, Father. If I survive my current mission, I will make things right with you. I apologize for the way I left things with you. Please know you are in my thoughts.

Your loving son

Had he not made it home after his mission? I wiped my cheeks which were wet with tears. I wasn't an overly emotional person, but I certainly understood regrets.

My phone buzzed in my pocket, and I pulled it out to see a text from my editor, Carrie.

A little birdy told me you've been slaying it at the literary festival. Congrats. But I need pages soon.

I laughed. She never liked anything that distracted me from writing. I sent back an emoji of a woman giving a salute.

While some writers might have been annoyed by the constant nudging, I needed the reminders. I could get lost in the weeds of research and real life at times.

I loved writing, specifically mysteries. But my attention span sometimes needed focus. My career would not have survived all these years without Carrie's constant nudging and understanding. She was much more than my editor. She was my friend.

I sat down at my desk and opened up the notebook where I kept notes on my work and James and Sebrena's cases.

Someone had wanted them both dead. They'd used poison, one that wasn't easily handled or used.

I wrote down the group of friends from the past. The mayor, Dr. Hughes, James, Keeley Boyle, and Chef Patrick were all friends back in the day. The book had loosely nodded toward each of them as a killer, except for Keeley, the victim. But there were only three of them that were possibly a murderer.

The book had to contain a clue, but I hadn't found it.

I doodled on the paper in front of me.

While I didn't think the mayor was the one who killed James and his agent, I didn't rule him out quite yet.

My best guess was Dr. Hughes. He would know how to handle the poison, which was an important part of the puzzle.

But why?

And who had the chef been fighting with after the banquet?

I glanced at my phone. It was late.

I'd forgotten about speaking with the headmaster Henry Charlton. The care home was west of town. I'd check with him the next day to see if he could shed light on the matter.

Mr. Poe barked.

I jumped. Then I hopped up to find out what was going on because he never left Lizzie's side once they had retired for the evening.

He was at the front door.

"What are you doing out of bed?" I asked him.

He growled at the front door.

I peeked through the peephole, but I didn't see anyone.

"Do you need to go outside? Let's go to the back."

He held his ground and growled again.

"Is someone out there?"

His growl became more guttural. Nerves snaked down my spine. But I was no wilting flower. I preferred to tackle trouble head-on.

I picked up the umbrella and held it like a weapon.

"Right then. Let's get this over with," I said as I opened the door.

FOURTEEN

Mr. Poe bolted out and barked as he reached the front gate. It was pitch-black because of the clouds above. I squinted and looked to the right and left. No one was there. But Mr. Poe was a very good boy. He didn't cause trouble unless he was worried about something.

Still, he could have been after a squirrel or rabbit. To him, the other small furry creatures that sometimes visited our garden were his nemeses. But he'd been quite upset, and I'd never heard him growl like that.

Had someone been in our garden? Soft rain fell, and I shivered. I popped open the umbrella to cover us.

"Come on, then," I said. "Whoever it was is gone. Good for you, trying to scare them, though."

I tried to convince myself it was a rabbit. We'd been warned that this time of year they could be a nuisance.

Inside, I grabbed a towel from my bathroom and dried Mr. Poe off. He sat there as if disappointed that we hadn't caught the culprit—but he was patient. Once I had him dry, he trotted upstairs and back to bed with Lizzie.

I smiled. He was a peculiar little dog, but I adored him.

Had someone been trying to break in though?

No. The court was as safe a place as there was.

Unless it was the killer.

But why would they be after us?

Because I ask too many questions.

My nerves were jangled. I sat back at my desk and opened my notebook.

The sooner I figured out who was behind this craziness, the faster life could return to normal.

The next morning, I woke to my sister clearing her throat.

I was at my desk and lifted my head off my keyboard. I glanced at the screen, which was full of nonsensical words and letters. My face wasn't a very good typist.

"You promised to make yourself go to bed and no more falling asleep at your desk," she said. "It's bad for your neck."

I blinked, trying to think back as to why I was here. Then I remembered Mr. Poe's intruder alert. I didn't want to scare her, especially if it had been a small animal.

I glanced at the book on the edge of my desk.

"I found some more of Grandad's letters." I pointed to the book.

"Oh?" She smiled. "Are they to our father?"

I shook my head. "I wanted to wait for you, but I read one from our dad that hadn't been opened. I thought we could go through them all together."

"I'd like that. Let me look at the one from our dad."

She read through it.

When she was done, she wiped her eyes with a tissue. "Do you think he didn't make it back?"

I shrugged. "I don't know. There's something I've been wondering since we moved here."

"What's that?"

"We both feel like someone is watching us from time to time, but it doesn't necessarily feel malevolent. What if it is our dad?"

Her head snapped up. "But why wouldn't he contact us? And why didn't he make things right with our grandfather?"

I sighed. "You're right. I've just been wondering."

She shivered. "It's weird that someone might be watching us, but you're right. We've both felt it. Maybe he has amnesia, or something like that."

I smiled. "You are starting to sound like a writer."

She chuckled. "I'll leave the imaginary scenarios to you. I want to look at the rest of the letters, but I've got to get to the store early. Caro and I had a rush yesterday before the banquet, and we need to restock."

"Do you need help?"

"No. We've got it covered. Some of the festival volunteers are coming in to help. Today, it's all about romance writers. They are the loveliest people. Some came in yesterday and spent a small fortune at the store. They brought us cake."

"Unlike we mystery writers who like to cause trouble."

She laughed. "You all are perfectly lovely, well, apart from he who shall not be named. By the way, you're going to give up on all of that, right?"

I couldn't lie to Lizzie. We were twins.

"Before we get to twenty questions, I need coffee."

She laughed. "Fair enough. I just worry about your safety. Our safety, really."

"Trust me, I understand. The last thing I'd want to do is cause trouble for you, Lizzie."

She scrunched up her nose. "Okay. Well, Mr. Poe and I are off to the store. Behave yourself."

"Always," I called out as she headed toward the door.

She laughed.

. . .

After a shower, one of Lizzie's cinnamon rolls, and three cups of coffee, I texted Kieran. He was at the station, so I headed that way with my notebook.

Sheila was typing on the computer but motioned me to the back of the station where his office was.

He was on the phone.

"Right," he said. "Can you pinpoint a time of death? Is there any way?"

His eyebrows went up. I sat down across from him.

"Do you have any idea when that will be?"

He sighed, and then hung up the phone.

"Problems?" I asked.

"Always. Dublin are still backed up. Celebrity or not, they don't really care. Unlike my bosses, who demand answers and aren't happy with excuses, like the lab is running behind. The superintendent is angry that there is so much media coverage and we have so little evidence. I keep getting the same run around from the coroner. They pinpointed the poison but can't tell exactly how it was delivered to the victims."

"I thought you said it was in the tea." I frowned.

"Right, but why did it take another twenty-four hours to work on Sebrena? Did they ingest it at the same time? These are things I need to know right now.

"Do you have something new? Did the book we found at James's cottage give you any more clues?"

I cleared my throat. "I talked with Lolly, and she said that Keeley left for America. So, the story in the book isn't true. It may have been loosely based on the group of friends, but the novel isn't exactly how it all happened. They helped her run off with her boyfriend and, apparently, she still lives there. I did a search for her but didn't find anything on social media. But maybe she didn't want to be found."

"True. Were you able to tell if James wrote the manuscript?"

I shrugged. "It could be a very early version of his writing."

"I spoke with Mrs. Byron who used to be the head librarian," he said. "When they were kids, that same group was accused of several crimes that happened around town. Including early manuscripts from some lesser-known Irish writers that had gone missing from the library archives.

"To this day, she was certain James and his friends took them. But none of those crimes were ever proven."

I pulled out my notebook. "Yes, Lolly told me a similar story yesterday. Of those friends, the mayor, Chef Patrick, and Doctor Hughes are the only ones left. Well, that live here in Ireland."

He sat back in his chair. "The mayor is a problem. It'll mean my job if I even hint he's a suspect. He's already blaming me for the two murders as if I committed them."

It was strange to see Kieran stressed. He was usually the calmest person in the room.

"I'm not sure why, but he likes me," I said. "I can tell him I'm doing research for something. But do we have any real reason to suspect him?"

"No. Other than being a part of that group, Doctor Hughes doesn't have an alibi for the murders. He lives alone and outside of town. He does have household staff who work for him, but they were off the day of the first murder."

"That feels suspicious, and the fact that he would know how to use the poison."

"But also kind of obvious. As if someone might be setting him up," Kieran said.

I blew out a breath. "True. Chef Patrick seems obvious, as well. I mean, jealousy is quite often a motive for murder."

"Right. Except, he has a decent alibi for each of the murders. He had kitchen help around him most of the day that Sebrena died. And his girlfriend said he was home the night James died."

"I'd feel better about life if we could figure out who is going around poisoning people. It's making me paranoid. Last night, Mr. Poe started growling like someone was on the other side of the front door."

"Was there?"

"Not that I could see. It might have been a small animal."

"Have you given yourself away? Who was the last person you talked to?"

"Why do you always blame me?"

"Because you aren't always discreet when you suspect someone."

He wasn't wrong.

"I spoke with the mayor and the chef. Oh, and I asked Doctor Hughes some questions during his class. So, all of them."

He frowned. "I told you to be careful."

"I was. What about James's home in Dublin? Did the police find anything?"

He shrugged. "I've been so busy with the evidence here that I haven't been through it all. They've logged everything."

"I realize I'm an outsider, but I'm a pro with research," I said. "I could help."

He shook his head. "I think you have *helped* enough."

"That's not fair."

He blew out a breath. "You have been helpful. I just do not like the idea of you tipping off the killer that you have found them out."

"I haven't done that," I said. "I can assure you. You have a small staff, and I'm sure a great deal of information to go through. It's just research and much safer than me interviewing the suspects, right?" Though, he couldn't keep me from doing that either.

"Put some files in a folder or on a thumb drive. I can review papers and photographs for you and flag anything interesting. I have some free time. Let me help."

That wasn't true. I should have been writing when I wasn't helping with the festival. But we needed to find the killer.

"You will keep insisting, won't you?"

"We've only known each other a few months, but you understand me well, Kieran. Just let me help, and I'll get out of your hair."

"And you will leave the interviewing of suspects to me?"

"Yes." Except for the appointment I'd made with the mayor. My plan was to tell him it was research for a book. As a fan of my writing, he'd already offered his expertise on political scenarios more than once. But Kieran didn't need to know about that.

Oh, and I still needed to speak with the former headmaster of the local secondary school.

He pulled a thumb drive from his desk and plugged it into his computer. "If you tell anyone I've done this, it will be my job."

"I'm the soul of discretion."

His eyebrows went up, but he moved files over. "I'm giving you half of the photos and all the manuscripts they found on his hard drive."

"What do you hope for me to find in the manuscripts?"

"That he wrote them all," he said. "I keep thinking, why kill a writer? We found the old manuscript at the cottage. But what if he plagiarized or hired another writer to pen his novels? I hear that sort of thing happens all the time.

"In the photos, look for any that may have Shamrock Cove residents in them. Some tie to what has been happening would be helpful. I do not expect anything to jump out, but one never knows."

It was something.

He handed over the thumb drive.

"This goes nowhere," he said, before releasing it.

"Agreed. Anything I find is for your eyes only."

. . .

After checking with Lizzie at the store to see if she needed my help, I headed home to number three. I made some coffee and then sat down at my desk.

My cell buzzed, but I didn't recognize the number. I let it go to voice mail.

A minute or so later, I listened to the message.

"This is Margie, the mayor's executive assistant," the voice said. "He'll need to cancel his appointment with you this afternoon. He has town business to attend to and hopes you understand." She hung up.

I noted there had not been an opportunity to reschedule for a later date offered.

He doesn't want to talk to me.

But why?

I turned my attention to the computer files I'd been given.

Research could sometimes be tedious, but this was delving into someone's life. I decided to go through the photos first. Some had been downloaded from James's phone. Kieran must have found them. There weren't many. Unlike most of us, James didn't seem to keep a photobiography of his life. There was the odd building or body of water on a trip, but that was about it.

A folder of photos from his home contained some older and slightly tatty ones, as if kept in a box rather than an album. Some of the reproduced ones were difficult to make out.

About an hour into my flipping through the photos, I stopped on one that had James as a young man with some other teens. It took me a minute to realize this was the group of friends Lolly had been talking about. I was able to place James, the mayor, and some of the others. But I didn't recognize a couple of people standing in the back.

I printed out the photos and circled the ones I didn't recognize. Then I continued my search for several more hours. By the time Lizzie had come home, I had printed six photos that I had questions about.

At least there wasn't a big banquet to attend. This evening, writers from various genres were to meet all over town to talk in individual groups. It was a chance for writers to network with others who wrote the same thing they did, and I thought it was a very good idea.

"You're working hard," she said from the doorway of my office.

"Just doing research. How was the store today?" I'd promised Kieran I'd be discreet. I didn't usually keep secrets from my sister, but I'd told the truth. This was research.

"Busy. I'm not sure what I'd do without Caro and the volunteers."

"I could have helped."

She shook her head. "We made it through fine. The romance authors we were working with today were just lovely. Their fans bought tons of books. I'm glad to have a night off."

"I am, too," I said.

"Except you're working."

I laughed. "True. Just catching up on some things."

"Is there anything you want for dinner?"

"I was thinking of heading down to the pub," I said. "It's shepherd's pie night."

Her eyes lit up. "Oh, you're right. Let me wash up, and I'll go with you."

I nodded. My plan was two-fold. One of the people who knew a lot about Shamrock Cove history was Matt, who owned the pub with his mom. He was a talented barista and bartender and was up on all the local gossip. He often joked it came with the job.

He was quite a bit younger than the mayor, but his mom would have been around back when James had lived here.

Between the two of them, I might get a better feeling for the group of friends.

A half-hour later we set out for the pub. Thanks to the festival, the place was packed. The only seats were up at the bar. We didn't mind. We sat down at the end of the bar and waited patiently for Matt to make his way over to us.

"How are two of my favorite people in the world?"

"Hungry," I said. "Please tell us there some of your mom's shepherd's pie left."

He gave us a dazzling smile. "Of course," he said. "Are we drinking pints or coffee tonight?"

Lizzie and I looked at one another. "Pints," we said at the same time.

"Aye, to be sure you've had some busy days," he said.

"That we have," Lizzie said.

He walked away, and my sister bumped my shoulder with her own. "Are you going to tell me why we are really here?"

She was way too observant for her own good. As my twin, it was impossible for me to hide much from her.

"I'm sworn to secrecy," I said.

"So, you're helping Kieran," she whispered.

I sighed. "I'm just looking through some things for him."

"So, the research wasn't for your book."

"How do you know these things?"

"You have a tell. It's why I always win when we play poker."

"I do? What is it?"

She made the zipper motion with her fingers across her lips.

"Unfair," I said.

"But if you're doing research on your computer, why did you need to come to the pub? Wait. Matt's mom. She'd be about the same age as the group you've been talking to."

"Maybe you should be doing the investigating." I rolled my eyes.

She frowned. "I thought you were done with all of this."

"Most of it really is just research. And we know that Matt and his mom are safe. I just need her to confirm a few things."

"Just promise you'll be careful."

"That's why I'm using my computer for most of this."

"Except we are here with lots of people around," she continued to whisper.

"I was curious what they were like in school," I said. "She would have been younger than them. It won't hurt to ask privately if she knew anything."

She rolled her eyes. "Fine. But it's too crowded in here for you to chat with Matt's mom with any privacy."

She had a point.

Matt set our pints in front of us.

"Mom's taking a fresh pie out of the oven. It'll be ready soon."

"That sounds great," Lizzie said.

Several people left at once and Matt gathered up a tub to clear their dishes.

"You're busy. Let us help with the clearing up," Lizzie said.

"No. I couldn't ask you to do that."

Someone at the other end of the bar was trying to get his attention.

"You've got a customer who needs you. We don't mind helping out," she said, reaching over the bar to grab the tub he held.

"Okay, thanks. Dinner is on me tonight then."

"That isn't necessary," she said.

"No arguments." He pointed a finger at her.

"Deal," I said.

"What are you doing?" I asked as we cleared off the tables.

"Getting you into the kitchen with Matt's mom," she whispered. She handed me the loaded-down tub of dishes. "Take this back and see what you can find out."

I smiled.

My sister was incredibly clever.

Now, to find out what Matt's mom might know.

FIFTEEN

The pub kitchen was filled with an array of wonderful smells from the shepherd's pie to a stew bubbling on the cooktop. Mary, Matt's mom, was plating something when I walked in with the dishes.

She glanced up and smiled. "Making you work for your dinner, my Mattie?"

I laughed. "My sister volunteered us to help. It's crazy out there."

"'Tis. And I'm grateful for it. Not so grateful that two of our servers are out sick though."

"Well, we're happy to help."

"You and Lizzie are a blessing. Just set those over by the washer." She pointed to a machine in the corner of the kitchen.

I did as she asked.

"Is there anything I can help you with?"

She nodded toward the stove. "Can you give the stew a good stir and turn the fire to low." The stirring was no problem. It took me a few seconds to figure out which knob it was on the commercial cooker.

Before I could ask her anything, she stepped out of the

kitchen with a tray of food. I couldn't hear what she said to Matt, but then she was back inside. She pulled two bowls down and handed them to me.

"Mind serving these up? I need to pull some bread from the oven."

"No problem," I said.

I used the big ladle to put the rich, beef stew, topped with mashed potato into the bowls and set them on the counter. My mouth watered at the smell coming from those bowls.

Once she put the bread on the workbench, she put the bowls on some plates and added slices of the warm bread to the side of the dish.

She moved like a master of the kitchen.

"Whew, we've caught up, thanks to you and your sister. How is the festival going? I heard that awful James Brandt was murdered. And that woman who worked with him. What's the craic?"

She stared at me expectantly. I was the one who needed to ask questions.

"Kieran is keeping things close to his vest," I said. "But you said awful. It sounds like you too had a run-in with James?"

She rolled her eyes. "I dated him for a week when we were in secondary. Mind you, I was three years younger than his crowd. I was naïve back then and stupid when it came to boys. And, if I'm honest, I was looking for ways I could disappoint the judge. God rest his cranky soul."

She made the sign of the cross.

Her overbearing stepfather had been a difficult man and she'd been a rebellious teen.

"None of us is terribly smart about boys at that age," I said.

"At first, I'd been flattered by his attention," she said as she put the dirty plates and glasses into the commercial dishwasher. She shook her head. "I played hard to get for months. Then he finally wore me down."

"What happened?" I asked.

"We went on a few dates after school for about a week. I think when it became clear I had no interest in giving him what he really wanted—he tossed me aside."

What he really wanted? "Oh," I said as her meaning became clear. "What a jerk."

"Aye, he was a gobshite. As were his friends. They were quite a strong clique back then and were ruthlessly mean."

"I'm sorry you had to go through that," I said.

She shrugged. "You forget I was living with the judge at the time. Nothing they could say would hurt more than that old coot. As you know, he could be cruel. But he made me tough."

"Had you seen James since then?"

"No, not until he walked into the pub the first night of the festival. I would never do it, but I did think about spitting into his pint. He didn't recognize me though. For that, I was grateful."

"I wouldn't have blamed you."

She laughed. "He was too busy arguing with that harpy he hung out with. The other one who died."

"Harpy?"

"Aye. She sent her white wine back because it was too dry. She was the one who asked for a German Riesling. She's lucky we even carried it. I thought my Mattie might throw them out they were such a nuisance. Some people never change."

"Maybe he should have tossed them."

"Nay, we've had worse bullies in here. If you tossed out all the arses, we'd have no business."

We laughed.

"Any reason why, other than he was jerk, someone might want to kill him or his agent?"

She shrugged. "He made many an enemy back in the day. I wasn't the only one who had a run-in with him. He went through half the girls in secondary like it was some kind of game to him. We learned to be wary of that whole lot."

"Do you know what happened to the woman in that group. I think her name was Keeley Boyle? Did she date James?"

"Nay. She and Patrick were close, but like brother and sister. He wouldn't have let James at her in that way. He was very protective."

"Oh?"

She nodded. "That was so long ago, but she was in some of my after-school teams and was the nicest of that bunch. When she disappeared, everyone thought the boys had killed her. I do remember that."

"Why?"

"I can't remember exactly," she said. "They made right bags of that, I tell you."

I wasn't sure what she meant. "Do you mean they messed up?"

"Aye. If they'd told the truth from the beginning, they could have saved themselves and the Garda a lot of trouble. It wasn't until one of them was accused of murder that they came clean and told the truth."

"I heard she'd run off to America with her boyfriend," I said.

"Aye, they were giving her time to get away with her beau, from what I can remember. She was in a wee bit of trouble. Something about some accounts at the university where she'd been working part-time. I believe she was cleared, or the Garda would have dragged her back. But that group had been involved in her cover-up."

Well, that was interesting. So, she hadn't been murdered, but she had been accused of a crime. I hadn't seen any of that in the newspaper clippings. I needed to head back to the library to dig deeper. That was if I couldn't find the files online.

A timer dinged.

"That will be yours and Lizzie's shepherd's pie. I made one fresh when I saw you coming in," she said.

I scooted out of the way so she could get it out.

Matt came in with a couple of order slips.

"I didn't mean for ya to kidnap her," Matt said as he looked from me to his mother.

We laughed.

"We were just chatting," I said.

"Aye, it was grand to have some company in the kitchen. But I'll not keep you from your dinner," she said. She put generous servings of the shepherd's pie on plates, along with some of the warm brown bread. Then she handed them to me.

"I'll talk to you later, Mary. Thank you for the background."

"No worries, luv. Let us know if Kieran shares anything with you."

"Wait, are you involved in the murders?" Matt asked. "Are you helping Kieran with his inquiries?"

"You've met me, Matt. I'm naturally curious about everything. I turn it all into my stories. And I can't resist asking questions. And you all know what Kieran thinks about that." It was the truth.

They laughed.

"Ma, did you tell her about when James and Sebrena came in the other day?"

"Aye, I did."

"Did you notice anything strange?" I asked him.

"Just that they didn't seem particularly happy to be in one another's company," he said.

"Oh?"

He nodded. "She griped about the wine she'd been served. But I think she was more upset by James Brandt. Never meet your heroes, right?"

"So, you're a fan?"

"Not anymore," he said. "They complained about everything and didn't leave a tip."

"Rude," I said.

"Aye. We were glad to see the back of them. I had no idea Ma knew James from her school days."

"He hadn't changed much, except age had caught up with him," Mary said. "It isn't nice to speak ill of the dead, but he was just as nasty as he'd been back then. And I feel like that ugliness comes right through the skin, I do. He was no longer a looker. If women were interested in him, it was only for his money."

"Tell us how you really feel, Ma."

She gave him a look.

I agreed, even though I hadn't known him when he was younger. I didn't understand how he'd been able to steal women away from the other men they dated. I never judged a book by its cover, but he wasn't the best-looking man. He'd been balding, slightly chubby, and his clothes were a few sizes too small. It was as if he hadn't been able to understand the man he had become.

And there was something else. His treatment of Matt made me wonder how James had been with his fans. I'd been thinking the killer might have been someone in his group of friends, but maybe I'd been headed down the wrong track.

I'd talk with his former friends, and then I could move on.

If he could alienate someone as kind and forgiving as Matt, who else had he offended?

And what did Sebrena have to do with any of this?

SIXTEEN

The next morning the rain bucketed down as the Irish liked to say. It was a fitting phrase. I'd planned to go to the library first thing, but I decided to put a few hours of writing in first. I swear it had nothing to do with the text from my editor asking about how things were going and the guilt that came right after I read it.

After a few hours, I called the care home to ask if it would be okay to visit Henry Charlton, but the news was disappointing.

"I'm afraid he had a fall yesterday," the woman at the other end of the line said. "They've taken him to the hospital in Dublin." She hadn't even asked if I was family before she gave me the information. Things were different here than they were in the States.

Then she hung up.

I sighed. I hoped he was okay. There was no way I could make it to Dublin and back in time for my festival duties. Besides, Mr. Charlton probably wouldn't want strangers poking around if he was in pain. Speaking to him would have to wait.

The rain had become a soft drizzle by the time I'd eaten a

sandwich for lunch. I put on my mackintosh, and wellies, and then headed up the hill to the old stone building that held the library. The head librarian made sure their collection of books was comprehensive and they had a great national system where they could get any book needed in a day or so.

To get out of the house, I occasionally took my laptop to work in one of the small cubbies available among the carefully arranged bookshelves. There were also plush chairs all around, and the library had beautiful stained-glass windows that rivaled the church.

The bookshelves were mahogany and went from floor to ceiling. Rolling ladders were used to access the uppermost shelves. It was one of the larger buildings in town, and I loved that Shamrock Cove supported such a wonderful library.

It was a book lover's dream. One of the great surprises of Ireland was that it was a very bookish country. Ours was one of many literary festivals and even the smallest of towns in Ireland had at least one bookshop and a library.

Mrs. Gallagher, the head librarian, was at the long wooden counter near the double front doors. Her bright-pink reading glasses hung around her neck on a matching chain, and her wild mass of gray curls framed her face. Today, she wore a T-shirt that read: *It's a good day to read a book* and jeans with embroidered flowers all over them.

My sister called her boho chic and very un-librarian-like. I had to agree. She once told me she was in her late sixties and had no plans to retire. She could have passed for forty. She claimed reading kept her young.

"Mornin', Mrs. Gallagher," I said quietly.

"I told you to call me Alana, lass. What brings you in today? Research or writing?" Her voice was a librarian's whisper.

"Research, but not the normal kind. I have a few questions for you. Do you have time for a chat?"

She nodded. "Give me just a minute to find someone to cover."

She texted something on her cell, and a minute later one of the other librarians arrived at the front desk.

"Follow me," she said.

We took a winding way to the back of the library and entered a break room. "This worked out well," she said. "I was gasping for a cup of tea. Can I get you something?" she asked as she turned on the electric kettle.

"I've loaded up on coffee today. I'm good."

She set about readying her cup and then motioned for me to take a seat at the scarred wooden table.

"What is it you need to know?"

"I'll need to make this a confidential chat," I said. "I'm helping the detective with his inquiries."

"Oh, interesting. Let me guess, you want to know about the stolen manuscripts from back in the day."

I nodded. "Were you working here back then?"

"Aye, I was an assistant here. And I can tell you that I know those kids took several of our most famous drafts. We had a break-in one night; not long after himself, James Brandt, had asked to view them. He'd been refused because back then you had to be over eighteen to view the items in the special archives.

"Could not have been more than three days later. They pilfered one from James Joyce and another from C. S. Lewis. The latter was on loan. It was quite the crime. They came in through there." She pointed to a small window at the other side of the room.

"What made you think it was James Brandt and his friends?"

She shook her head. "Because they were the very manuscripts he'd asked to look at. Thick as thieves they all were," she said. "Even though the police searched their homes, nothing was found."

"And nothing was ever proven?"

"Nay. I was so furious because I knew those kids had them. I've no idea how they were able to hide them, but they did. We thought they might have taken them to sell them, but that never happened. Then, about ten years ago, the two manuscripts were shipped here anonymously. The police tried to track down who had sent them, but they'd covered their tracks well."

"That's strange. Maybe one of them had a crisis of conscience. What can you tell me about that group?"

"Brandt was a smart one. Did well in school. But there was something about him that..."

"What?"

"There was something off about him. Never did trust the fellow. He was the ringleader and acted like the world owed him something."

"And the others?"

"Are you asking me to disparage our mayor? He's in control of our funding, so I shan't."

I smiled. "That confidentiality goes both ways," I said.

When the kettle clicked off, she stood to make her tea. She sighed as she sat back down.

"I'll say this—our mayor isn't above doing a favor for a friend. I like to stay on his good side for that reason."

"Okay, what about the woman from the group who went missing?"

She nodded. "Right, Keeley lives in America or Canada now. I sometimes wonder what really happened back then. I've never believed the cover story that they were helping her escape a bad home life. She was at university and was doing perfectly fine on her own. I've always thought something bad happened the night they were celebrating. But, like I said, they were tight-lipped back then."

I pulled out my phone. "I find it strange that Keeley was the name of the missing woman in the manuscript the police found at Shamrock Cottage."

"I hadn't heard about that. What can you tell me?"

"I'm only telling you because I wondered if the manuscript might have been stolen. It was very amateurish. I was curious, since you're familiar with James's work, if you think this might have been one of his early manuscripts."

She put her reading glasses on and flicked through the document on my phone. Then she shook her head. "It could be him, but the style is quite different. We have some of his early drafts in the archives in Dublin. I can ask for a transfer if you'd like to compare them."

"Do you mind?"

She smiled. "It's my job. We haven't had any other manuscripts stolen. So, it isn't one of ours. Do you think this book has something to do with Brandt's death?"

I shrugged. "It was on the table with a draft from his current work."

"Do you think he plagiarized or used it as source material? I've kept up with his career through the years since this is his hometown. He's been sued more than once for words he's written."

"Again, I have no idea. Other than they were both mysteries, there is nothing that links them. And the style seems quite different, as you can see. I was hoping maybe you'd be able to tell if it could have been one of his earlier works."

She frowned. "I wish I could help, but I'm as clueless as you. He uses a much shorter chapter style, and the writing is quite different. But you're right, it is strange that it was found where he died. It could be. Let me get those early manuscripts he donated years ago, and we can compare. It will only take a few days."

"Thanks," I said.

She sipped her tea, and then pursed her lips.

"What is it?" I asked.

"He wasn't the only one interested in writing back then. Part of what brought that group together was their interest in books. They spent a great deal of time here working on and researching their books."

"The whole group?" I asked.

She shook her head. "Not the mayor. But Finneas was working on something non-fiction. It had to do with plants. Keeley was working on a romance. And Patrick was working on a C.S. Lewis biography. They all fancied themselves quite the literary set."

"Wait, Patrick was a writer?"

"Aye, though back then he didn't go by Patrick. He was Mark back then."

One of the boys I didn't recognize in the photo had been a skinny young man with wire-rimmed glasses and ill-fitting clothes. He looked nothing like the handsome chef. In the newspaper photo, he'd been somewhat bookish with long hair and bangs that nearly covered his rounded spectacles.

"Do you know why he changed his name?"

"I think I remember him saying in an interview that he preferred Patrick. But I think he was trying to get away from those early photos of himself. He underwent a makeover when he was on a British cooking show years ago. That show helped launch his career."

How had I missed all of that? "If he's so famous, why is he catering our literary festival?"

I hadn't meant to say the words out loud.

"You'll have to ask Lolly that, I'm afraid. Though, there was a scandal a few years back concerning one of his restaurants."

"Oh?" I'd also missed this. It was evident I needed to do a deeper dive on this group.

"He was sued for some reason, and it cost him a great deal

to clear his name. I can pull some of those old court records for you."

"Thanks."

She glanced at her phone. "I should get back to the desk. Let me know if there is anything else I can help you with, okay?"

"Thank you. I'll take a look at those court records, if that's all right."

"Of course."

A few hours later, I left the library with even more questions. I stopped by the station to tell the detective everything I'd learned, but he was out.

"He should be back in a few, if you want to wait," Sheila said.

"That's okay. I'm due at my sister's shop to help out. Just tell him I stopped by."

She nodded, and then went back to her computer.

On the way to the bookstore, I tried to make sense of everything I'd read about Brandt and his former group of friends at the library. With the exception of the mayor, others in the group had all been in some sort of legal battle, including the professor. His had been over his wife's estate. It turned out she'd been quite wealthy, and her family had blamed him for her illness, but nothing had been proven.

And she'd left everything to him in her will.

It was interesting that they'd all been writers back in the day. That strange manuscript had to have something to do with all this.

But I was more confused than ever as to why that might be.

SEVENTEEN

As I walked toward the bookstore, I happened to see the mayor and Chef Patrick talking just outside one of my favorite establishments, Paisley's Bakery. Named after the owner, who always had an array of delicate pastries, cakes, pies, and just about any other dessert one could imagine. I only allowed myself to visit once a week. It was that tasty.

The two men walked inside, and I followed. I planned to do some eavesdropping, but Paisley caught my eye as I entered. "Two times in one week? I feel honored, Mercy."

There were several people in line, and they all turned to look at me, including the men I'd followed inside.

"I'm breaking my once-a-week rule for a writing emergency. My next chapter needs some of your chocolate croissants."

Everyone laughed as if that made all the sense in the world.

She went back to helping the customers in line.

"I'm surprised to see you here, Chef Patrick."

He gave me a charming smile. "Why is that?"

"Because I figured you could make pretty much anything you wanted."

"True, but my pastry chef has a cold, and Paisley volunteered to help with the vol-au-vents for tonight's event."

"I know those have been on the *Great British Bake Off*, but I can't remember what they are." That was a lie. I only wanted him to relax and talk to me.

"It's a puff pastry with a filling, right?" the mayor asked.

"It is," the chef said. "These will be filled with creamy chicken. She made some early for me to try."

"Do you have a favorite here?" I asked the mayor.

He patted his belly. "A few too many favorites, but I'm always partial to a custard tart. I saw you go into the library earlier today. Are you busy doing research?"

I nearly choked and had to clear my throat. Why would he take notice of where I was going?

"Uh, yes. I'm working on a new book." That was the truth. "I heard a story I'm thinking about incorporating into one of my books. Actually, you two could help me out with that."

"How is that?" the chef asked. His eyes narrowed suspiciously.

I shrugged. "I heard something through the grapevine. You know how small towns are. It was a story about some missing manuscripts. I saw you two were thought to be involved back in high school. But I know you'd never have anything to do with that."

Way to just lay it all on the table. If one of them was a killer, I'd probably put myself in their crosshairs.

The mayor bristled. "Of course not. I'm an upstanding citizen and always have been."

The chef rolled his eyes, and it was all I could do not to laugh.

"Oh, I didn't think you were," I said. "I thought maybe you could give me some background on the theft since you were both living here back then. And why did the authorities single you out."

"Well, that was James's fault," the mayor said. "And if anyone took those manuscripts, it was probably him. I'd heard they'd been returned so I don't see how that is much of a mystery for you."

"Well, the idea came to me when we found James that day. As terrible as it all was, I noticed a couple of manuscripts on the table of the cottage. From what I understand, the police haven't been able to identify the writer of one of the manuscripts I saw that day.

"And I have a writer's brain, so it's been whirling with ideas ever since."

"I hadn't heard that," Chef Patrick said. "Wouldn't those have belonged to James?"

I shrugged. "Again, we were so caught up in finding him that I didn't really look that closely. I'm sure the police are checking them out. My brain is always thinking of scenarios when I find any sort of mystery."

A look passed between the mayor and chef, one that told me they had a secret they were not about to share.

"Sorry, we can't help you." The mayor's attitude was brusque, as if he wasn't happy with my digging.

Crud. What was it about that manuscript that made him so bristly? "Like I said, just my writer's brain going in a million different directions. I've been making notes for a possible new book. This always happens when I'm about halfway through my current work in progress. My brain wants to work on something new. I hope I haven't been too much of a bother. I just thought since you two knew James, you could give me some background."

The two men looked at one another again, and then the line moved up.

"What exactly is it you want to know?" Patrick asked.

"Well, from what I heard, he was quite popular in high school, and you all were the cool kids' group."

They laughed, which was a step in the right direction in calming down the situation.

"I don't know about that," Patrick said. "We would probably be called bookish these days. We were all obsessed with the literary world."

"And for James, women," the mayor interjected. "It was a game to him, and I'm afraid he broke a few hearts."

I smiled. "I'm sure you did as well. I saw the pictures from back then; you were, and are, all quite handsome."

The mayor's cheeks went pink. "Thank you for that." He seemed to settle down. "We were just kids, though. I'm guessing you are trying to lead us into what happened with Keeley?"

I blinked. "Oh, right. The woman from your group everyone thought was missing. Yeah, what happened exactly?"

The bakery had gone quiet, and it was as if everyone wanted to hear that answer.

"She was just trying to get out of a bad situation with her family," Patrick said. "We helped a friend, end of story."

Then he and the mayor turned around as if to say, that was enough of my prying.

"Right, but from all accounts, her parents were worried sick. And they didn't seem like awful people."

The mayor sighed and turned back. "They weren't. But they didn't approve of her beau at the time and were forcing her to move back home from the university. And someone in the department where she worked in the university planted evidence to make it look like she'd committed a crime. She hadn't. But the police didn't seem to care.

"We were all young and loved her dearly. We gave money, mind you it wasn't much back then."

"And we bought her a plane ticket," Patrick added.

"Then we stalled the authorities, so she had time to make her escape," the mayor finished.

"That was kind of you. Were the police able to prove her innocence?"

"Aye," the mayor said. "When she disappeared, they took a harder look at some of her co-workers and found the person skimming the accounts. She was no longer under suspicion."

"And you've all stayed friends through the years?"

Once again, there was a glance between them.

"We haven't seen her in years, and she's never come back to Ireland," Patrick said.

"But the four guys, you all stayed friends?" I asked as if I hadn't a clue.

The mayor frowned. "As people grow older, they often grow apart," he said. "As I've mentioned before, I kept up with James's career. But once he left town, he never looked back. No one was more surprised than we were that Lolly and her committee convinced him to return."

He would have been better off if he'd ignored their invitation, but I didn't state the obvious.

They were next in line, and the conversation dropped. I hadn't learned much, but from their faces I judged that they absolutely had helped James steal those manuscripts. Both had cut their eyes to the left and down. I hadn't missed that tell, which might have indicated guilt, anger, disapproval, or all three. They didn't like that I'd called them out.

By the time I'd bought the croissants I didn't need, but would totally end up eating, the two men were nowhere to be found.

I only hoped they didn't figure out they'd moved to the top of my suspect list, along with Dr. Hughes. The good doctor was doing a book signing that evening at the store, and I wasn't going to miss an opportunity to chat him up again.

· · ·

At the store, Mr. Poe was behind the counter staring up at Lizzie with adoration. She was busy packaging books, but she gave me a quick wave. "Mr. Poe needs a walk. I left his leash in the office," she said.

I headed to the back of the store. I couldn't help but stare at the cabinet that held the secret doorway to the storage area. It was hard to believe it had only been a few days since we'd found Sebrena's body in there.

I still didn't know if we were dealing with one killer or two. Nor did I have any solid evidence as to who might have done the dastardly deeds. Though my gut, which I trusted, had narrowed down the list to the group of friends who had a falling out in the past.

A few minutes later, Mr. Poe and I were on our way to my favorite walking path. The wind blew bitterly off the sea, and it was bracing. But it cleared the cobwebs of tangled thoughts clouding my brain. We were several feet from the cliff's edge when I noticed a strange plant.

"Do you think that's it?" I asked Mr. Poe.

He cocked his head as if he were thinking about it.

I was no botanist, but the plant looked like the picture I'd found of cuckoo-pint, which was what had been found in James and Sebrena's systems.

"I can't believe it just grows out here where anyone might touch it."

Mr. Poe moved a little closer to sniff the plant, but I pulled him back gently. "We need to stay away from that one, boy. The berries at the bottom of the plant are extremely poisonous."

As if he understood every word, he backed away.

I smiled. "You really are the smartest fellow I've ever met." I scratched him under his chin, and he licked my fingers. But then his body went rigid.

He yapped softly.

I glanced ahead to see someone coming toward us on the

cliff's path. We were close to the edge, and I backed away to put a few feet between us and the boiling sea below.

"Thanks for the warning, little guy," I said.

When the figure came closer, I recognized him.

Dr. Finneas Hughes wore another tweed jacket with jeans and wellies. He carried a worn leather journal in his hand. He was staring down at the ground, and I didn't think he saw us.

"Hi, Doctor Hughes," I said.

His head snapped up in surprise.

He pointed his pen at me. "You're that writer."

"Guilty," I said. "I wondered if I could ask you a quick question."

He nodded but didn't look happy about my interruption.

"Is that cuckoo-pint?" I pointed to the plant at the cliff's edge.

He frowned but his gaze moved to where I'd been pointing. Then he walked over to it. "You didn't touch it, did you?"

"No. I remembered that you said it was very poisonous."

"'Tis," he said. He took his glasses out of his jacket pocket and then he bent down for a better view. "Harmless to birds, mind you. But all parts are harmful to animals and humans."

"Right. So, if someone were to use it as a murder weapon, how would they go about it?"

He stood and turned toward me. "One would have to know what they were doing to avoid poisoning themselves. It needs a delicate touch. Locals grow up knowing never to touch it. Getting rid of it is nigh impossible. If the whole plant isn't dug up, even small parts will propagate. Why do you ask?"

"I heard a rumor that the plant was used to killed author James Brandt. He was a friend of yours, right?"

He blanched as if I'd slapped him. "What?"

"You were friends?"

"No. What you said before—he was poisoned with arum maculatum?"

"If that's the same as cuckoo-pint, yes."

He shook his head. "Impossible. You must have it wrong. I heard a bookcase fell on him."

"I found him, and it did. But someone had also poisoned him. They aren't certain yet how the poison was ingested." I knew it was in the tea, but I didn't want to share that much.

Kieran would be angry that I'd mentioned the poison, but I did so to gauge his reaction. He'd seemed completely surprised.

His eyes were wide, and his jaw hung open in disbelief. "How do you know this?" he asked suspiciously.

I couldn't tell him I was helping Kieran with the investigation. The only reason the detective allowed me to assist was because I'd promised to keep things mum.

"I was at the station and just happened to see the post-mortem file. Please don't tell the detective I peeked. He'll kill me. But I'm a writer and I can't help but be curious. Besides, I'd been thinking the bookcase was an odd way to die and I wondered if there was more to that story." That was the truth.

"I don't understand. There are much easier and safer poisons to kill someone." He didn't seem to realize what he'd said. "A person would have to be willing to take a great risk to use it. Strange. Strange." He looked down at the plant again. "No. It does not make sense at all."

He shook his head and then took off walking down the path toward town.

"Bye," I said.

But he ignored me.

"Well, he certainly seemed surprised by the news," I told Mr. Poe. "Maybe we move him down on the suspect list."

Mr. Poe gave a small yap.

On the way back to town, my mind whirled with ideas.

It wasn't until Mr. Poe growled, which he only did when he sensed danger, that I stopped to pay attention to my surroundings.

I glanced around us.

"What is it, boy?"

A chill shivered down my spine. We were at the fork in the path at the edge of the cliff. One way led to town, the other down to the sea.

But no one was there.

I gently tugged on Mr. Poe's leash. "Come on, boy, let's get back to civilization."

My stomach churned with nerves, and I'd learned to trust that feeling when I'd lived in NYC. Had my stalker followed me here? Or had I just given too much information to a murderer?

I wasn't waiting to find out.

The botanist had seemed worried and thoughtful when he left. Did he know who the killer might be? If so, would he be next on the killer's list?

EIGHTEEN

The backroom of the Crown and Clover pub had high church ceilings and a lot of space. The room had been set up with several round tables and wooden chairs. This was a cocktail mixer for attendees who had donated a certain amount to the literary foundation the festival was raising money for, and these were people who loved books.

All of the authors who were presenting and signing at the festival were in attendance.

"Before we open the doors to the attendees we would like to thank you for your contributions to our festival," Lolly said from the small stage that had been set up. "Those who will be here tonight donated a great deal to the foundation. While the numbers are still being counted, so far we've made double from the last festival. I can't tell you what that means for those who benefit from the foundation. Children and adults deserve the right to read. And the contributions tonight have helped fund many of the programs in place to make that happen."

Literacy was a cause close to my heart. I'd donated a chunk of my last advance anonymously. Lolly was right. Everyone deserved the opportunity to read. Something that many of us took for granted, kept others from jobs that would improve their lives.

I glanced around for my sister, but I didn't see her. I pulled out my phone and texted to see where she was.

She didn't answer.

Maybe she's busy.

She'd told me she would meet me here because she had to chat with committee members. Most of them were here, including our friends Rob, Scott, and Brenna. I went over to them.

"Have you seen my sister?" I asked.

"She and Mr. Poe had a mishap with a puddle, and she had to go home and change," said Scott. "Eejit that I am, I was supposed to let you know but totally forgot."

I let go of the breath I hadn't known I'd been holding. I was extremely protective of my sister, and she of me. We were all each other had left in the world.

"He does like to jump in them," I said.

"Yer wee man was covered head to toe in mud. She said he'd been acting strange all day as if he were trying to tell her something."

I blamed myself for that. He'd been unsettled after our run-in with the professor on the cliffs. I'd thought he would settle down once he was with his favorite person, Lizzie.

"If only he could speak, it would make life easier," I joked.

They laughed.

"That's exactly what your sister said," Rob replied.

I smiled. We did tend to think alike.

That explained why she hadn't answered me yet. She was probably giving him a bath.

"Is everything going okay with the festival? She said you had an emergency meeting."

"Aye," Brenna said. "We talked about the media attention surrounding James's death. Some of the reports don't show us in the best light. We were talking about ways to distance ourselves from what happened, while being respectful of those who died."

"Oh? And what did you decide?"

"Nothing," Rob said. "We can only continue to promote the upside like tonight, where readers get their one-on-ones with their favorite authors. And we've chosen to ignore the rest. If we respond, it only adds fuel to the fires that are already burning out of control, to use a cliché."

"That makes sense, though. Hopefully, the readers will have fun tonight and post enough positive reviews to outweigh the negatives."

"We can only hope," Scott said. "Though, we've already had more sign-ups for next year than we've ever had at this point for previous festivals. I think everyone is worrying for no reason. A week from now, the media will move on to something else, and no one will remember what happened here."

Having dealt with the media in the past, I had to agree. At home, the news cycle for a famous death was probably less than twenty-four hours.

"Speaking of which, any news you can share with us?" Rob whispered the question. "Or anyone you want us to chat up?"

Scott shook his head. "Kieran will yell at her if she shares anything. Right?"

I nodded. "Though, if you can keep a secret, I could use some help keeping an eye out for a couple of people. But you're right, if Kieran finds out he'll kill me."

"We are the souls of discretion," Brenna whispered. "You know that."

She wasn't wrong.

I glanced around to see that Lolly was still on the other side of the room. Her loyalty would always be to her grandson Kieran, which was only fair. But he wouldn't be happy if he heard what I was about to say.

I told them about the school group. Their eyes went wide.

"The mayor is so... I can't imagine him being involved in any sort of theft," Rob said. "He's such a rule follower."

Rob had been trying to get his food truck up and running before the summer tourist season, but had run into a roadblock with city hall. They were making him jump through hoops because Shamrock Cove had never allowed food trucks before. The mayor felt they had to proceed carefully, so that they didn't have to allow just anyone a license.

"Please understand, I'm not asking you to speak to any of them. Just if you see them talking to one another, perhaps eavesdrop."

They smiled.

Rob rubbed his hands together. "Oh, I love being involved in the snooping."

"Two minutes until the doors open," Lolly said over the loudspeaker. "Authors, please find your station. The tables have your names on them. And be prepared to sign books. One of the only complaints we've had this year are the long lines at book signings.

"Though, I consider that good news. Since the attendees made a sizable donation to be here, we want to cater to them as much as possible."

"Go to your table." Rob shooed me away. "We'll keep an eye on the suspects for you."

Chef Patrick and his team had set up a banquet of appetizers on the wall nearest the stage. I'd wait until after the mixer to eat. I didn't want to risk spinach in my teeth. And maybe I wasn't super excited to eat food made by a possible suspect.

Kieran had mentioned Patrick had alibis for the murders, but I just didn't trust him. Maybe it was that he was too handsome.

Tonight, he had a scowl on his face, and his eyes were on the mayor.

I wonder what that is about?

I didn't have much time to think about it. A minute later, the doors were opened, and my table was swarmed by readers.

"Are you okay?" a woman in her late sixties asked me.

"What do you mean?" I smiled as I took the stack of books from her and set them down on the table. I motioned for her to sit next to me. More readers took seats around me.

"We heard you found the bodies," a man said next to her.

"This is my Alfie," the woman said proudly.

"And this is the love of my life, Aileen. We've been married for fifty-seven years. And one of the things that keeps us together are books. We love 'em, including yours, miss."

"Congratulations. That is a very long time, and I love that you share books. It's lovely to meet you both."

"Thank you, lass. So did you find the bodies?"

I'd hoped to steer them away from that. I was determined to be the soul of discretion. Well, except for telling our closest friends.

I nodded. "Unfortunately."

"Poor man," Aileen said. "And bless your soul. Is it true he was murdered? And that you'll be using it for one of your books."

"No, I'll stick with fictional stories, and I'm so glad you enjoy them," I said.

"'Tis so exciting to learn about the behind-the-scenes," Aileen said. "And to sit next to an author we've admired for so long. We love all of your books."

My cheeks heated with warmth. I'd learned long ago not to base my self-worth on what others thought of me or my work, but that didn't mean I couldn't enjoy the kind comments that came my way.

It was a few hours later before the room started to clear out. I'd fielded a couple of questions about James, but most people wanted to discuss my books. Talking with those who were passionate about novels made time pass quickly. And it was funny how the fans recalled small details I'd long forgotten.

I was exhausted, but also excited to get back to writing. Hearing how much someone enjoyed one's work never got old.

"This is the last call," Lolly said. "We will ask the attendees to exit. Authors, please stay behind."

As the room emptied, I looked for my sister. She was nowhere to be found. Nor were any of my neighbors, except for Lolly.

Where was everyone?

I pulled my phone from my pocket.

She'd never answered me.

My twin instincts kicked in, and my stomach plummeted.

Something was very wrong.

NINETEEN

My stomach churned with nerves as I made my way home. As I walked, I kept hitting Lizzie's number on my cell, but she didn't answer. My heart in my throat, I pushed open the door to the secret entrance to the court. Everyone's porch lights were on, and the neighbors were in our front garden.

"What's going on?" I asked as I jogged toward them. "Where's Lizzie?"

Rob held up his hands. "Breathe, she's okay. No one was hurt."

"Hurt? What happened?"

Sheila, who had just come out of my front door, motioned to me.

"Kieran needs to see you," she said.

"How is my sister?"

"She's fine. They're in the kitchen with Mr. Poe. He scared off the intruder."

"Intruder?"

I rushed inside. "Lizzie?"

"Kitchen," she said. Her voice was calm so at least there was that.

She and Kieran sat at the table.

She jumped up when I came in and we wrapped our arms around one another.

"Someone broke into the house."

My heart sped so fast I could barely breathe.

"Did they hurt you?"

She kept her arms around me but shook her head. "Mr. Poe scared them off. They ran out the back as we came in the front."

I glanced down to find Mr. Poe staring up at us as if confirming her story with the cock of his head.

"Good boy," I said.

"He scared me to death; he has no fear," she said into my shoulder. "I was worried the person who broke in might hurt him. But he chased them away."

He was such a tiny furball, I couldn't imagine anyone being scared of him. But he did have a ferocious bark and growl.

"I'll need you to look through your office to tell me if they took anything," Kieran said from the table.

"What?" I'd forgotten he was there.

"According to your sister, the only room they seemed to have searched is your office," he said.

My head swung around so fast to Lizzie it made my neck hurt. "Laptop?" My life and my latest book were on that small machine. My heart dropped to my stomach, and nausea threatened. Everything was backed up to the Cloud, and I emailed my story to myself every time I finished a chapter. But my life was on that machine.

"Still there," she said. "Though Kieran said it appeared they were looking for something. You'll need to check it out."

"To see if they took anything," Kieran added. "Forensics is in there now, searching for fingerprints. We have yours on file, but we will need yours, Lizzie. You can come to the station tomorrow."

"Okay."

"But I'd like to take you into your office, Mercy, to see if anything is missing."

I nodded, still nervous. My stomach churned with fright and anger. How dare someone break into our home? This wasn't the first time it had happened here.

We had an intruder not long after Lizzie and I had moved to Shamrock Cove, but it was a killer looking for information. That was scary enough. But when I'd lived in Manhattan, my stalker had broken into my apartment more than once. The intruder hadn't done much more than move things around, but they had taken some personal items like photos, and one of my old journals.

The police couldn't do much, and not long after that, Lizzie needed my help in Texas. We'd received the news about our mom's cancer diagnosis, and I'd dropped everything and gone home.

After Mom died, Lizzie's fiancé and his daughter had been killed in an accident. We'd needed a fresh start.

One of the reasons we'd moved to Shamrock Cove was because it was one of the safest places to live. It truly was. I guess we were just unlucky.

Or it might have had something to do with my nosing into murder cases.

I followed the detective to the door of my office. Papers had been strewn about. Drawers were open on my desk, and some books had been pulled from the shelves. I let go of the breath I'd been holding when I found my laptop still plugged into the large monitor I used when writing.

Like most authors, my laptop was my life. I was glad it hadn't been taken.

I glanced around the room taking in the contents. The only thing that was missing had been next to my laptop.

"Well?" Kieran asked.

"The copies of the manuscripts you made me are gone," I

said. "I'd been locking them up, but forgot and left them out. But that doesn't make sense. They have to know you have the originals from the crime scene. What good would it do them to take the ones you made for me?"

"Perhaps they thought them to be the originals," he said.

I shrugged. "I don't know. What if they, too, are looking for information within the text."

"What do you mean?"

"Maybe they needed copies of the two manuscripts because they are trying to find something out."

"Or trying to hide something," he said.

"You could be right, but like I said, they have to know you have the originals. I've read both manuscripts front to back. I didn't find any clues." And it had been extremely annoying.

"You said the story was about a missing girl," he said. "The older manuscript, I mean."

"Right. But we know that James and his friends helped someone get to the States and away from their family. She wasn't really missing. There's no reason to take the manuscript since it's a work a fiction."

"Is there anything else missing?"

I looked around the room. Then I shook my head. "I don't think so. It almost looks like they knocked the books on the floor to make it look like more than it is."

Anger roiled in my stomach. Maybe it was petty, but I'd never liked strangers touching my things. I wasn't sure anyone would like that. But something niggled at the back of my brain.

"You have that look," he said.

I stared at him, puzzled. "What do you mean?"

"The one where you've come to a conclusion of sorts."

"It's not really a conclusion so much as an idea. What if they took the manuscripts on purpose to steer us in the wrong direction? We've both been through them, and found nothing."

"Except we still don't know who wrote the original book. The one that wasn't published."

"True. But it almost feels like the killer wants us to think this is about those books. What if it's a ruse?"

"So, you don't think they took the books for a reason?"

I scrunched up my face. "It's just all way too convenient and contrived. If this was in a novel I was writing, my editor would beat me up for it. No. I think it's someone who knows what a red herring is. And they are most definitely trying to send us down the wrong path with the investigation."

"So, they broke into your home for no reason? It seems odd they'd chance it, given how secure the court is."

"Right. Did any of our suspects live on the court in the past? Maybe their parents and someone in the family inherited the home?"

"Not as far as I know. My grandmother might know more about that. But it hasn't come up in our research of the victims or suspects. We do know they came in the back door, which was unlocked."

"They came in the back door? That means they knew about the path that runs along the back of the homes."

He smirked. "That's public land. Everyone knows about that path."

He wasn't wrong.

At one time or another, all of the suspects had lived in Shamrock Cove. Our tiny neighborhood of thatched cottages was well known in town.

But if I was right, someone was determined to manipulate us into thinking that the deaths had been tied to something in the manuscripts. If they weren't, we would be back to square one.

Or, would we?

The mayor, the professor, and the chef were our suspects.

They all had reasons for wanting James dead. He hadn't been the best of friends. But why would one of them kill his agent?

TWENTY

The next morning, I tidied my office and cleaned up the fingerprint powder that forensics had left behind. I doubted they would find any prints other than mine or Lizzie's. The criminal who had pulled off the two clever murders would not have left fingerprints behind.

I couldn't help but wonder if he or she might be trying to throw us off the trail by breaking into our house, unless it wasn't the killer at all.

I shivered. *No. It's not possible.*

But perhaps, given the publicity around the literary festival, it was. My appearance at the festival and the fact that I now lived in Shamrock Cove had been well publicized. Then there were the news articles online about me possibly killing James.

Had my New York stalker crossed the pond?

Lizzie and I had both experienced the feeling that someone had been watching us since we arrived in town.

"No. I will not let whoever did this win by making me scared in my own house." I refused to let my mind go there.

I'd just settled at my desk to write when my cell rang. I may have jumped a little.

"Kieran, what's up?"

"Gran said you'd wanted to speak with the headmaster. He's back at the care home, and I wondered if you might want to go with me to ask him questions."

"I—sure." I was surprised he'd asked. Most of the time, he wanted me to stay away from the investigation unless he needed my expertise on something.

"Meet me at the station at a quarter past." He hung up.

The clock on the wall showed I had fifteen minutes. I hurried to pour my coffee into a travel mug. I went back to my office and pulled out the stack of paper I'd printed at the library when I'd been doing research on James's old friends.

At least the intruder hadn't taken those. Though, he or she probably hadn't noticed the papers on the printer or Mr. Poe had scared them away before they could grab them.

There was one photo in the newspaper of all the friends together. Just in case the headmaster needed faces to put with the names, I thought it might be helpful.

I grabbed my jacket. I made sure the house was locked before heading out of the court.

"Everything all right?" Rob asked from his garden. The day was sunny and bright. He wore a large straw hat and gloves. "We were wondering if the police found anything."

I smiled. Of course, he and the rest of the court would be curious. That and everyone looked out for one another here.

"Nothing yet," I said. "But you'll keep an eye out for us?"

"Of course. And sorry for your trouble. I know that has to be unsettling—having a stranger in your home—again." His tone indicated he was quite sincere.

"Thank you," I said. "I feel better knowing you're right next door."

He smiled and waved me off.

When I hit Main Street, it was quite crowded. With our home behind a giant stone wall and set away from the town's main drag, it was easy to forget the crowds. We'd been told it would be even busier when the summer tourists came to visit our beautiful beaches.

Fans stopped me a few times on the way to the station, making me about five minutes late. But when I finally arrived, Sheila motioned for me to go back to Kieran's office.

He was finishing up a phone call and waved me to come in.

"Thank you for letting me know," he said. And then he hung up.

"Sorry, I'm late."

"I've been on the phone with the coroner."

"Oh?" I sat down across from him. "Is there any new information?"

"Both victims had the tea we found on the scene in their stomachs."

"Which means Sebrena lied about going to the cottage the night James died."

He nodded.

"Do you think she killed him and accidentally dosed herself? According to Doctor Hughes the cuckoo-pint plant is extremely dangerous."

"If that was the case, she would have absorbed it through the skin, and there are no rashes or anything to indicate she touched the plant. And why would she drink it? It would take a deft hand to hide the poison in a tea."

"You make a good point. Are you thinking it's the botany professor? He's the only one who might know exactly how to do that. Though, I can't see his motivation. And believe me, I've been researching all of the friends."

"As have we," he said. "I'm not willing to point the finger at anyone until we gather more evidence."

"Silly proof," I joked. "That's all you think about."

"Funny how that works, as I am a detective. Should we go see what the headmaster has to say?"

"Yes. About that, I was surprised you invited me."

He smirked.

"What?"

"I invited you because he loves books and writers."

"Oh, then I should be flattered."

"Aye. And he isn't my biggest fan."

I jerked my head back in surprise. "Why is that?" I followed him out the door.

"My ma and pa sent me here to live with Gran when I was young. I'd become a bother, and they thought she'd set me straight. Turns out they were right. But it took some doing, and the headmaster had no patience for my shenanigans."

I shook my head. "You seem so... by the book. It's difficult for me to imagine you as a troublemaker."

He laughed. "I was a mess. But my parents had been right about Gran. Between her, the judge, and your grandfather, I was soon set on the proper path."

"I knew about the judge. You mentioned that at his wake, but I didn't know about my grandfather. I don't think I realized you knew him that well."

"Aye, everyone in town did. He was a good man and had a way with people. Even dumb kids like me. He's the reason I started reading comic books and manga."

I coughed. "You read manga?" I always associated the art form with young kids and a special breed of young adults who grew up with anime of all sorts.

"Aye. I'd loved the animated films and television shows growing up. Once your grandfather found this out, he carried a wide selection in the bookstore. The idea, he said, was that if I were reading, I wouldn't get in trouble."

I laughed. "I still can't imagine you as a bad kid."

"I wasn't bad," he said. "Just had a need to cause some trouble. But being here in Shamrock Cove, where everyone knows your every move, it wasn't so simple. My parents were right to send me here. It was probably the best thing that ever happened to me. It's tough to get away with mischief when everyone knows exactly who you are, and who to call. It only took a few ear-twistings from Gran before I decided to change my ways."

I smiled. "It's my first time living in a place like this, and it does feel like people take the time to get to know you much faster."

I was used to the coldness of New York, where you could be lying on a sidewalk, and people would just step over you. And that wasn't an exaggeration. New Yorkers had seen more than most and tended to ignore everything around them.

"So, my being here is a buffer for you."

He snorted. "Aye. The headmaster has a sharp mind and never forgets a transgression."

I smiled. It was odd to see the detective intimidated. I couldn't wait to meet the headmaster.

The care home was up the hill past the church and off on a side road about two blocks down. Like most of the buildings in town, it was at least three hundred years old, but had been built onto. The builder had tried to match the stone for the one-story annex, but it was still obvious which part was newer.

Inside, the scent of antiseptic mixed with bleach was powerful. After Kieran showed his credentials, we were ushered into a lounge area where residents played cards, watched television, or simply read in cushy chairs and sofas. I'd never seen so many walkers and canes in one place.

"The director asked that you wait for her here," the receptionist told us. "She will take you to Mr. Charlton's room."

The residents glanced up from what they were doing as if curious to see the new arrivals. A few of them waved at Kieran and smiled. He waved back. They eyed me with curiosity, and I grinned. I loved the older generations, there was great wisdom in their eyes.

"Hey, ho, Kieran good to see you," a black woman in her forties said as she approached us. She wore a set of scrubs with a name tag that said Deirdre Abebe.

He held out his hand to shake hers. "It's good to see you, Deirdre. This is Mercy McCarthy. Sorry to be a bother, but we need to ask Mr. Charlton a few questions for background on a case."

"Aye, he's expecting you. We just got him settled, though. I'd appreciate it if you kept the visit short."

"Not a problem," Kieran said.

"I've read your mystery novels," she said to me as we followed her down the hallway.

"Oh?"

"I recognized you from your book covers. You look much younger in person."

Kieran and I laughed.

"Thanks, I think," I said. "My friend Brenna took new head-shots for me, so those will go in the next book."

That had been Brenna's suggestion since she agreed with the care home manager about my current bio picture making me look older than I was.

"Books are a blessing," she said. "I love my job, but escaping into a good mystery helps me deal with the sadness we often face here. So, thank you for all the years of entertainment."

"Thank you for taking care of the seniors in our society. I would not have the patience."

She laughed. "You have no idea."

As we turned down another hallway, she held out a hand for us to stop.

"Fair warning," she said. "He's in one of his moods. Was not happy with us for sending him to the hospital after his fall. But as I explained to him, it is procedure."

"Was he hurt?"

She shook her head. "He's fine. A few contusions, but nothing serious. He doesn't like using his cane or the walker, but hopefully, now he will. He fell hard and scared us to death."

She knocked on the door, and there was a grumbling answer inside.

"Like I said, he's in a mood. Though, he's often like that. Good luck to you. Don't stress him too much more. The doctor said he needs his rest."

"We'll be quick," Kieran said.

She opened the door and ushered us inside.

This wasn't like any nursing home I'd been in before—not that I'd been in very many. There were floor-to-ceiling windows, room enough for a living area and bedroom, and even a flat-screen on the wall. The volume was so loud it hurt my ears, and the news played on the television.

"Mr. Charlton, you have some visitors. Our own detective inspector has brought a guest with him," Deirdre said as she turned the television off.

The former headmaster was dressed in a cardigan that had leather patches on the elbow and brown slacks. Under the sweater, he wore a mock turtleneck. He reminded me of a character from a Dickens novel with his well-carved features and haughty air.

He sat in a wingback chair near the window. His room was decorated with an assortment of antiques and art.

"A guest? No one said anything about a guest," he grumbled. Then he turned slightly, and stared me down.

"I've been looking forward to meeting you," I said. "I understand you have a great historical knowledge of Shamrock Cove and its residents."

He seemed to ponder that for a moment. "I suppose I know more than most," he said grudgingly. "I've heard about you. The American writer whose sister has reopened Driscoll

O'Heynes's bookstore. I suppose you are doing some research into our fair town. But that doesn't explain why the trouble-maker is here."

It was all I could do not to suppress a grin. *The trouble-maker indeed...*

"I'm here in an official capacity," Kieran said. "We need to ask you a few questions."

"You trying to set me up for a crime? I have been in hospital."

Kieran sighed. "No, sir. We need background information on some of your former students."

The man's eyes narrowed. "And are you in the habit of needing the help of famous American writers to do your job?"

He stared pointedly at Kieran.

The detective ran a hand through his curly hair, which he often did when he was frustrated.

"Ms. McCarthy is a consultant with the department and has helped explore the literary aspects of the case." To his credit, Kieran kept his voice level and didn't give into the older man's insults."

"Literary aspects?" He turned his gaze to me. I sat down in the matching wingback chair across from him. Through the window there was a great view of the cobbled street below. "What do you want to ask me?" he said to me.

"When I found the body of James Brandt, there were two manuscripts on the table. One appeared as if it had been written years ago. Since you knew James and his friends when you were headmaster, we thought you might be able to give us some insight into them. And, perhaps, you might know some-thing about them that might help with the investigation."

He frowned. "Why would I know anything about a manuscript?"

"I apologize, I didn't mean about the manuscript. I meant

were they troublemakers like the detective?" I meant it as a joke, but neither man smiled.

He harumphed.

"They were far worse than Detective Inspector O'Malley. He never harmed others. His pranks were more a cry for attention, I'd say."

I glanced up to find Kieran staring out the window, but there was a slight blush on his cheeks.

"But James and his friends were cruel?" I asked. "At least, that is what I've heard from some of those who were in school at the same time."

"Aye, that's an excellent word for them. We did our best to keep them separate, by making sure they did not share classes in the curriculum, but outside of school, we had little control over the miscreants."

"So, you weren't a fan of James."

"Nay, he was the worst of them. Do not get me wrong, he had a brilliant mind. But he was walking trouble, and they all covered for one another. That made it nearly impossible to punish them for their deeds, but we all knew what they'd done."

"That is why we are here," I said. "I wondered if, perhaps, you knew of someone that might have wanted to get back at them. Maybe someone they pranked, who years later wanted to get even."

He shook his head. "We're talking about murder," he said. "While they were awful teenagers, I can't imagine anyone would do that."

"Can you give me some idea of the pranks they did? Maybe some of the worst ones you can remember."

"I remember them all," he said. "My body may be feeble, but my mind is as sharp as ever."

"I didn't mean to say otherwise." I smiled.

"Sir, we're only interested in those cases where perhaps

someone was so embarrassed they would hold a grudge all these years later."

"You two are not listening. Those boys were too clever to get caught. While we suspected them of many things, we could never prove their part. And those they pranked, as you say, weren't talking for fear of retribution, I'm certain. But that James, that one was rotten to the core. I know people liked his writing, but he was a terrible human being."

I blinked. No one had come out and said that, though I was certain many of the people we'd talked to believed the same thing. I'd seen how he treated my sister and the fans. He wasn't a very good person.

But why had someone murdered him?

I told the headmaster about the manuscript we'd found.

"I wouldn't be surprised if it was loosely based on their exploits," he said. "Though James was not the only writer back then. They all were well-read lads and part of what kept them together was they wrote books. I can't imagine they would have been very good though."

"So maybe it wasn't James who wrote it?"

"You'd have to ask his friends. Though, even now they might not tell you the truth. Deceitful bunch, more than any crew we ever had at the school."

"What do you think about the mayor?" I asked. "Do you think he could have written it?"

Mr. Charlton rolled his eyes, and I couldn't help but laugh.

"Least talented of all of them and not terribly bright. I can't imagine he could string more than a few words together. I'm told his assistant writes his speeches. She's Agatha's granddaughter, who lives next door. His family had money, and I'm certain that was the only reason they let him be a part of their group."

I didn't know the mayor well, but the speech writing didn't surprise me much. He seemed a man who enjoyed his position of power. And while he pretended to be welcoming and cordial, there was something about his demeanor that had never sat quite right with me.

Though, I often thought the same about most politicians who had any sort of power. I'd met a few in my world. Some were down to earth and perfectly lovely humans. Most believed too much of their own hype.

The mayor was too interested in being popular. But would he have killed his friend to keep something in the past from coming out into the open? And what would that have been?

"Is there any information you might have that could help with the investigation?" Kieran asked.

The elderly gentleman glanced up at the detective as if he'd forgotten he was there.

"As I said before, I knew them long ago. I can't imagine any of my students would hold such a grudge as to commit murder. We taught you all better than that." His gray eyes narrowed.

"But they were clever enough to tamper with school records," he said. "That's something we could never prove, but we knew it was them. I was always surprised by Finneas's success as a professor."

"Oh? Why is that?"

"He barely skated through with his studies. His only interest back then was science and computers. He nearly failed at everything else. I was always certain he was the one who hacked into the school's database and changed the grades. We'd only put them on the computer a year before. Those machines were still new to us.

"He was smart enough to change everyone's marks so as not to draw attention to his friends. I always thought he'd end up in jail, but he was a clever hacker."

That surprised me. Finneas Hughes didn't seem the hacker type at all. He was the cliché professor with his patched-elbow sweaters and jackets. He reminded me more of the headmaster who sat in front of us.

They had been in school years ago and I always thought of hacking as something that happened in the last twenty years. But computers had been around for far longer.

I'd made the number one mistake an investigator shouldn't. I'd assumed, from his current job and behavior, that he was a certain type of person.

"There is a rumor that James and that woman he worked with were killed by poison, is that true?" he asked.

I glanced up at Kieran. I knew better than to say, yes.

"I'm not at liberty to say," Kieran gave his pat answer. "The investigation is ongoing."

Henry seemed to think on this and turned back toward the window. "Well, if it was poison, Finneas would be your man. I've followed his career at the university and into the private sector. He's become quite the expert. And the one class he did excel at was chemistry. He had a propensity for creating reactions with his concoctions. But he and James were best friends. I can't see him harming him." He yawned. "I'm an old man, and I need my rest."

With that, he closed his eyes. Kieran motioned for me to follow him out.

"What did you think?" I asked as we neared the entrance to the home.

"He didn't give us much, though I didn't know about the hacking," he said. "I'll need to follow up with the professor on that."

"Could I go with you?"

He gave me a look.

"Call it research. I use poison a great deal in my books. It's always interesting to talk to an expert."

"You can be honest with me, Mercy."

I sighed. "Fine. I like being part of the investigation. There. Does that make you happy? Now, can I go?"

"Yes. But it's more about keeping you safe than anything. If I don't take you with me, you'll go out on your own."

I still might.

Now that I had some history about the mayor, I had a few more questions for him—questions I didn't think he'd answer in front of the detective.

TWENTY-ONE

When we hit Main Street, Kieran's phone went off. He paused to answer, and I stood a few feet away to give him privacy. The street was crowded with festival attendees. I pulled the schedule out of my pocket to see what was happening over the next few hours. It was non-fiction day for the festival. Several readings were happening at the bookstore.

"I need to head back to the station. Promise me you will not visit the professor until I can get away."

I shrugged. "I'm headed to the bookstore to see what's happening there," I said. It wasn't exactly a lie. It wasn't my fault there was a hundred percent chance I'd run into the professor before his reading.

And being the friendly person I was, I'd probably strike up a conversation.

The sunshine from earlier in the morning had disappeared. A soft rain fell, and I pulled the hood up on my coat. Walking down Main Street, I caught someone watching me.

I turned to see who it was across the street, but there was no one there. Well, there were people strolling down the sidewalk, but no one indicated they had even noticed me under the awning of Linda's old store.

Great. Now I'm losing my mind and becoming paranoid.

At the bookshop, the readings took place on the second floor, and I helped straighten the chairs for the professor's reading, which was scheduled for twenty minutes later.

When he came up the stairs, he seemed flustered.

"Is everything okay?" Lizzie asked.

He was pale and out of breath.

"I don't know," he said. "Someone tried to run me over."

Lizzie's jaw dropped.

"What?" I asked.

"I was on the road by the cliff, and a motorbike nearly did me in. I could have fallen to my death." His hands were covered in mud, as were the knees of his slacks. He'd definitely taken a tumble.

"Lizzie, call Kieran," I said.

"On it." She pulled out her cell.

"Did you recognize who it was on the motorcycle?"

He shook his head.

"They wore a helmet with a face shield. Everything happened so quickly. The bike was black, and everything the driver wore was the same color. It was all a blur."

I motioned for him to sit down in one of the chairs meant for the audience.

"Was anyone else around?" The streets had been packed when I'd come into the bookstore. There had to be witnesses.

"No," he said. "No one but me near the cliffs."

"Okay. Maybe someone saw them come through town. Did you maybe see a license plate?"

He shook his head. "I was in my head. I always am when I walk. By the time I registered there was a motor close by—I'd been shoved to the ground, so close to the edge of the cliff I thought I was a goner."

He grew paler by the second.

"Take a deep breath," I said. "You may be in shock."

He did as I asked, and I sat down opposite him.

"Is there anyone who might want to cause you harm?"

He shook his head and then stared down at his shoes. "In the past, I had many students who were not happy with me. Since my wife died, I keep to myself," he said. "I tend my plants and write my books."

"What about someone from your past?"

He frowned and glanced up at me. "What do you mean? I just told you I don't teach anymore."

"I meant further back. Like when you were in school here. I heard rumors about the group you hung out with in secondary. You all were kind of wild. Maybe someone who lives here has a long memory."

"We were all kids back then. No one cares about that now." He stared at me like I'd lost my mind.

I wasn't so sure about his past. "You say that, but then someone killed James and his agent. And then they just tried to shove you off a cliff."

"I—you think it has something to do with James?"

"Yes," I said honestly. "Is there anything from your days back then that might have made someone want to kill him? Or knock you off a cliff?"

"No. Yes, we were all friends. And we got up to trouble now and then. Most boys do at that age. But there was nothing we did that would warrant murder years later."

"And yet, someone is after you. What about your recent past?"

"I told you, since leaving the university, I live quietly."

"Okay, what about the mayor or Chef Patrick?"

He scoffed. "Two friends I've had for most of my life?" He

stared down at his hands. "You know the mayor would put you in jail for throwing that sort of aspersion his way."

"You probably aren't wrong about that. Please know I'm just trying to help you. There is no telling what the detective inspector will think, but I believe your troubles are tied to James's death. The problem is figuring out how. I don't know that you and the others from your group have been exactly honest with the authorities. It's too much of a coincidence."

There, I'd said it out loud. He could think what he wanted.

"You have to be wrong. It was probably some kid up on the cliff."

I sighed. "But what if it wasn't, Professor? Think about it. One of your friends is dead. By your own admission, had the culprit pushed you harder, you would have gone over the cliff. You have to know something."

"What makes you think that? Have you discovered a clue?"

Yes. But I wasn't about to tell him that.

"Kieran's on his way," Lizzie interrupted. "I'm going to get you a cup of tea."

"Thank you," he said. "I need to clean up."

His hands shook, and he grabbed the back of the chair when he stood.

"Right. Follow me," Lizzie said. She crooked his arm in hers and guided him to the restroom that was on this level. We were lucky enough to have two in the bookstore.

"Would you like me to cancel your reading?" she asked as they walked away. "Everyone will understand if you need us to."

"That is kind of you. Can you give me a moment to sort myself out?"

"Of course. You let me know what you want to do. We still have plenty of time."

After he'd gone through the door, I turned on my sister. "I was trying to get him to talk."

"The poor guy is in shock," she whispered. "He was growing paler by the moment."

I pursed my lips. "I saw that, but he has to know something. His friend was murdered, and someone just tried to shove him off a cliff."

"Which is why you should leave the questioning of the victim to me," Kieran said behind me.

Oops.

Later that evening, I helped my sister and Caro straighten the shop. We were exhausted when we headed to the pub for a poetry slam. I was curious if it meant the same thing in Ireland as in the States.

The pub was crowded, but the owner, Matt, had reserved our table for us with a sign. "I feel so special," I said as he led us through the crowd.

"Well, you are my favorite writer, and your sister gives me a major discount at her store. So, only the best for you two."

We laughed.

"Black and tans?" he asked.

Lizzie and I nodded.

"How about you, Caro?"

"I'll take a Sullivan's Irish Gold," she said.

"Coming up. Chips will be coming out hot soon. Do you want some?"

We nodded.

"So, have you figured out who killed the author and his agent?" Caro said bluntly.

I'd just taken a swig of water and nearly sputtered it across the table.

"Why would you say that?" Lizzie asked.

"Oh, it's all around town that you two are helping the police with their inquiries. And Kieran was in the bookstore today. Did you find out who tried to kill the professor?"

We hadn't said a word.

"Again, who told you that?"

She smiled. "You two don't seem to understand how small a village Shamrock Cove is. We have a town full of gossips. It's the favorite pastime among our residents."

"Did you know that group of friends?" I asked her.

"I'm a little bit older," she said. "But I knew of them. They spent a great deal of time at your grandfather's bookstore. And while they had a reputation for being rude, they weren't with him. He demanded respect but in a quiet sort of way."

We never knew him, and we were always looking for more information that would help us get to understand him better. So far, we'd learned that he was kind, generous, and at the same time, had a strained relationship with our father. Another man we knew little about.

"Were they as big of troublemakers as people say?" I asked.

She laughed. "Yes. Though they covered their tracks well, especially the mayor."

"Oh?" Lizzie seemed surprised.

I wasn't. He had that politician's demeanor. He was as fake as they came. On the surface he seemed affable, but behind the scenes I'd seen the trouble he'd caused for Kieran with the investigation.

He refused to talk about his friends. And he probably had the best insight to all of them. But he still played that game of covering their backs, even though one of them might have killed James and his agent.

"Can I ask you something completely off the record?"

Caro shrugged. "I'll answer if I can."

"You know that gang fairly well," I whispered. "If you had to pick one to commit murder, which one would it be?"

Her eyes went wide. "Do you really think it was one of that crew?"

"As a mystery writer, I'm keeping my options open."

"She has trouble keeping her nose out of ongoing cases," Lizzie said.

I made a face at her.

"I try to help if I can. It's not like I mean to make a nuisance of myself."

"And yet..." she said.

"Mean," I countered.

She giggled.

"I've never trusted the mayor," she said. "I certainly didn't vote for him. He's always given off a certain attitude like he's entitled to the world. I'm sure that comes from having parents who own a fair amount of Shamrock Cove, but I've never cared for him."

"Do you think he's capable of murder, though?" Lizzie whispered.

I had the same question.

"Yes, but he'd probably hire someone. I know that is awful to say. But I can't see him getting his hands dirty. And he was great friends with James, at least from the outside looking in. He was always talking about how the author had come from our wee village. He was quite proud of the fact."

"What about the others?" I asked. "The caterer, Patrick, or the professor."

"I hadn't seen Patrick for years," she said. "From what his ma says, his business in Dublin has been doing quite well. There were even write-ups in magazines about him. Though, he had some trouble a few years ago with the law. I can't quite remember."

I was still waiting for the articles the librarian Mrs. Gallagher was getting me. I could probably find them on one of the databases I used. I made a mental note to look later.

"I don't know much about the professor," Caro said. "He's one who keeps himself to himself. He ordered a great many books through the store, though."

I'd heard that he was a hermit more than once. He didn't seem the type to commit murder, but he was the only one who would know exactly how to use the poison.

"He did enjoy chatting with your grandfather," Caro said. "He used to come into the store about once a month. And we always kept a selection of the books he wrote in the store. He's quieter than the rest of them, though. What happened to him this afternoon? Did someone really try to kill him?"

"Kieran's on the case," I said. "Someone definitely ran Professor Hughes off the road."

"He might have died by falling off the cliff if he hadn't caught himself," Lizzie added.

"That is frightening," Caro said. "To think we have another murderer in our wee town."

"Do you remember back in the day? Maybe there was someone they offended that might want to get back at them?" I asked.

She grimaced. "They weren't exactly well-liked. And most of what I heard back then were rumors. Like I said, they were quite adept at covering for one another. That way they couldn't be blamed for their misdeeds. There are any number of young women who might have wanted to kill James. But I don't know why they would kill his agent."

I had been so focused on the set of friends, that I hadn't thought much about those they'd caused problems for in the past. But Caro was right. It would make sense for someone on the outside of the group to want them dead.

Probably more so than one of them knocking each other off.

Darn. The festival would be over in a few days, and we were no closer to finding the killer.

There was a commotion at the door and people waved at the person coming in. It was the mayor.

He wore a fake smile as he shook hands.

My thoughts tumbled through my brain. There was just something about the guy that rubbed me the wrong way.

Maybe he wasn't responsible for the deaths, but I couldn't help but wonder if he knew who might be capable of murdering his friend.

I just had to figure out a way to ask him without ending up in a jail cell.

TWENTY-TWO

The poets at the slam were more entertaining than I could have ever imagined. While there were a few serious ones among the crowd, several of them offered up funny poems or limericks that were apropos for a pub crowd. Throughout the night, I kept a close eye on the mayor.

When he was on his fourth pint, I decided to make my move.

Lizzie's twin instinct must have kicked in when I stood. She grabbed my hand and shook her head.

"I'll only be a minute," I said as I pulled away. First, I went to the bar and asked Matt what the mayor was drinking. Then I ordered a pint and took it to him. There was a twenty-minute intermission before the next poet went on the small stage in the corner that Matt had set up.

The mayor sat with his friend Patrick, the caterer. And there were some women sitting with them that I didn't recognize from the village.

"Evening, Mayor," I said. "I was headed this way, and Matt asked if I'd bring this over to you, his treat."

He had that glassy-eyed look of someone who was already two pints past his limit.

"Well, this is a first," he said. "I've never had a famous author wait on me." He said it in the creepiest of ways, as if I might have been interested in him.

Ugh.

"It's crowded, and I'm just helping a friend," I said. "Did you hear someone tried to kill Professor Hughes earlier today?" I almost snorted. Not the best conversational segue.

"What?" The mayor stared at me like I was crazy.

"Wasn't he a part of your high school crew, along with Patrick here?"

The mayor blinked.

Patrick opened his mouth and then shut it. His eyes narrowed. "What are you saying exactly?"

"Nothing," I said. "It's just that you guys might want to be careful until the killer is caught."

"You think the same person who knocked off James and his agent are after us?" the mayor asked. Then he laughed hard. "You really do have a writer's imagination."

He was an annoying jerk.

"What about the professor? Someone tried to knock him off the cliff."

"And yet, he survived," the mayor said. "The detective said it was an accident. They are trying to find the motorbike. You're seeing some kind of conspiracy where there is none."

"So, you don't think the person who killed James and his agent might also be after the rest of you?"

They laughed again as if that was the funniest thing they'd ever heard.

Then they glanced at each other and guffawed even harder.

Why couldn't they see what was happening?

Probably because they were drunk.

"This is why you should stick to writing fiction and leave the real crime investigations to the proper authorities. I assure you our good detective inspector has it all well in hand."

It was all I could do not to call them on their ignorance. I forced a smile on my face. "I'm sure you're right. Kieran is very good at what he does."

"Are you using all of this to write a book?" Patrick asked. "Is that why you have so many questions?"

I shrugged. "I don't normally use true crime stories," I said. "But yes, there are elements here that I may use in a future book. Like a mysterious manuscript that no one seems to be able to place. At first, Kieran thought it was an old one of James's. And there is a rumor that he may have illegally borrowed some manuscripts, and it might be one of those. The problem is, there is no name. Do you guys know anything about that?

"You know, to help me flesh out my story."

"You should be careful in throwing out accusations about the dead," the mayor said, anger in his voice. "James didn't need to steal other people's work. He was quite a talented author and well-regarded in these parts."

"That he was," Patrick added. "And my friend here is right. You better not be spreading these rumors about theft around. James was one of Ireland's greatest talents."

It was all I could do not to say that C.S. Lewis, James Joyce, Samuel Beckett, Oscar Wilde, and Maeve Binchy, to name a few, were far better. And much more famous.

The two men clinked glasses. The women from the table joined them.

Feeling foolish, I just walked away. I'm not sure what I thought I might accomplish by tackling the pair of them head-on.

They'd certainly closed ranks.

But they'd also threatened me, and I hadn't missed that.

They were still at the top of my list.

. . .

By the time I woke up the next morning, Lizzie had already gone to work at the bookstore. She'd been angry with me for drawing the attention of the mayor and the chef.

"If they are the murderers, you just put a big target on your back," she'd said as we walked home. Then, she refused to speak to me.

She wasn't wrong.

I had the day off from the festival, as today was dedicated to those who wrote children's books. Several students from schools in the many towns surrounding Shamrock Cove would be visiting the festival free of charge.

I planned to stay away from those crowds. It wasn't that I didn't like children, I did. I just wasn't fond of too many people in small spaces. And just for today the festival attendance, thanks to those school children, would quadruple.

I much preferred the coziness of my office with a fire going as a soft rain fell outside.

I read through the notes of my manuscript to remember where I'd left off and where I was headed next with my mystery.

I forced the thoughts whirling in my brain about the professor, the chef, and the mayor out of my head. My gut swore that even if they hadn't committed the crime, they had something to do with it.

"Stop it," I said out loud. "You have to finish your book."

But my brain refused to cooperate.

Then it hit me, for once, I could use AI in my favor. While I wasn't a fan of AI companies using our published books to further their database capabilities, there was a way to use it.

Even though the copy had been stolen out of my office, I had taken photos of it in Kieran's office. I had enough to type in several sentences and to do a search. My hope was that the words might signify a specific author. While I was well-read, I hadn't read all the books in the world.

After typing in some of the sentences from the early pages of the manuscript, I hit search. I wasn't sure why I hadn't thought of doing this earlier—except it had been a busy few days.

The search left me with several links. When I clicked the first one, I gasped. The link led to a book written by a Keeley Boyle-Henley, the same name as the member of James's gang in high school who had run away to America.

"Could it be the same person?" It had to be.

After ordering the digital version of the book, I clicked on her website. She'd written several thrillers, and the one I'd found in the search had been the last one she'd written.

The message on her website read: *It is with a heavy heart that we let you know our dear Keeley has gone to write with the angels.*

She was dead.

I did another search for her obituary. She'd only passed away a few months ago, but there was no reference to how she'd died.

Keeley was survived by her three grown children, a husband, and a few grandchildren. She'd been living in the small town of Mountain View, Arkansas. I'd been there once for a book signing. It was a conclave of artists surrounded by beautiful mountains and trees. And not at all the backwater town I'd expected.

I searched for newspaper articles surrounding her death, but there weren't any—only the obit.

There was nothing about her death being investigated, but I still wondered. Was it a coincidence that her death came so close to James and Sebrena's?

Could someone have killed her? Did the authorities even know to look? While Mountain View was fairly progressive in the arts, they might not have had the medical resources to check for poisons.

I checked to see who her publisher and agent were. I had an idea but my editor, Carrie, wasn't going to like it very much.

"Here goes nothing." I dialed her number.

TWENTY-THREE

As I suspected, Carrie wasn't happy with my request. I sat at the desk in my office, and her silence on the other end of my cell spoke volumes. Still, I needed her help, and I had a feeling if I made her as curious as I was, she might just do what I needed.

"Look, you're a pro at getting information from people. I'm just asking you to reach out to her agent and ask how she died. Though, maybe not so bluntly."

Still nothing.

"Are you there?" I asked.

"Mercy, you've asked me to do some strange things over the years, but I'm not sure what you expect with this. How do I make it so that I'm not some macabre lookie-loo trying to find out dirt?"

She had a point.

"Blame me," I said. "Tell her agent I was a big fan and when I found out about Keeley's death, I was heartbroken. And that I wanted to know what happened to her."

Carrie sighed on the other end. "I thought you were supposed to be working on your book, not another case. You would think after nearly getting killed the last time that you'd stay out of police business."

She had a point. My sister felt the same way.

But Sebrena, James's agent, had been killed in our bookstore. Even though we weren't suspects, I wanted the world to know we had nothing to do with her death. Also, someone had broken into our house and that made it personal.

That, and there was the fact that Kieran had asked for my help with the manuscript. Finding out more about the author would help our investigation, I just knew it.

"This time the detective inspector asked me to help. That's why I'm curious about the book. We found what has to be an early draft of her last novel during our research. It's strange that she waited so long to tell that story. The draft we have is at least twenty years old, probably more, given she went to the States in the late 1990s.

"So, it isn't just morbid curiosity. You'd be helping with the investigation. And if you could find out any information about this last book she wrote, we'd be even more grateful."

"Is this the super-hot detective Lizzie told me about?"

"When did you talk to Lizzie?"

"Last week, she said you were working on your book. I hope that is true."

"I can't believe you've been checking up on me. But why were you two talking about Kieran."

She laughed. "Because I asked if there was anything distracting you from your work. And she said as long Mr. Hottie didn't come up with a new case for you to investigate, that you should be solid. I should have known he'd come up with something."

"I'd like to remind you that a woman died in our store. You saw some of the messages on social media. I just want to help find the real culprit to clear our name.

"And it's not like that with Kieran. We're just friends and professional colleagues."

"Right."

I sighed. She wasn't going to believe me no matter what I said. Even though she was a jaded New York book editor, she was a romantic at heart.

I mean, Kieran was attractive, but our relationship was nothing more than two professionals putting their heads together. And yes, while neither of us would admit it, we enjoyed spending time together.

"So, you'll call her agent for me?"

"Fine. But that book better be in by the deadline. Or I'll come to Ireland and stand over you until it's done."

I laughed because she would absolutely do that if she thought it necessary.

"I knew I could count on you."

We hung up. While I waited for her to call me back, I skimmed the novel that had been published. While there were similarities to the original manuscript, enough so that I knew she was the one who wrote it, the latest version was much more professional and polished.

It did focus on a group of friends who covered up a murder and got away with it for years. That is until one of the suspects found out he was dying and wanted to set things right. The others killed him to keep the truth from coming out, but they weren't careful about it.

The detective in the novel figured out what they had done and was able to prove it.

I made notes. It was odd that the suspects were a professor, a politician, an author, and a famous chef.

That had to hit home with her group of friends. The book had come out just a few weeks before her death.

It was all too suspicious.

I called Kieran, but it went to voicemail.

I waited for the beep. "No rush, but when you get a chance, can you come to number three? I think I may have found a link, and possibly another murder."

Hopefully, that message would make him curious to stop by soon.

An hour later, I was in the kitchen getting some coffee and a snack when my cell rang loudly in my pocket. The ringtone for Carrie was a giant foghorn, and it made me jump.

"What did you find out?"

"You owe me," she said. "Now I have to take the agent out for lunch."

"Order something nice?" I said and laughed. "Sorry."

"You should be. Okay, so she said that Keeley's heart gave out. That she'd had a birth defect, so it hadn't come as a surprise. There was no autopsy, though."

My jaw dropped.

"Did you tell her about what was happening here?"

"No. It wasn't my place. I called on your behalf, and that's what she believes. She's actually sending me an autographed copy of the latest book for you. I hope you feel bad about that."

I did. "She could have been murdered, and no one would be the wiser."

"Is that your writer's brain coming up with a story, or is it based on fact?"

"You know it's an assumption, but I am going to tell the detective inspector that he should look into Keeley's death. If she was killed, that means the murderer is on a spree covering up something. She would be his third victim, well, actually his first. And someone tried to shove the professor off a cliff yesterday."

"Wait. What? Mercy, promise me you are being careful."

"I am. I promise. I'm sorry I made you call the agent, but the information is incredibly useful, so thanks."

There was a knock on the front door, and I might have jumped for the second time that day.

"Someone is here. I need to go."

"Promise me you're working on your book," she said. Her tone was exasperated, and I didn't blame her.

"I am. I won't miss my deadline."

I peeked through the peephole in the front door and was relieved to see Kieran. Not that I was expecting the killer to show up and knock.

"I've been helping wrangle the children in town, and I need to get back to it. This better be important," he said quickly.

"It is. Do you want a coffee?"

"You know the answer to that is always yes."

I laughed. He was just as big a caffeine addict as I was.

As I made him a cortado, I told him everything I'd just found out.

"You can't jump to conclusions," he said. "We need facts."

"Right. I get that you need proof, but it's too much of a coincidence, right? What I don't understand is why the book would be the catalyst for all of this. As far as we know that group of friends didn't actually kill anyone."

"True," he said.

"Unless, it was Keeley that was coming clean. She had a heart condition. Maybe she knew she didn't have long, and she wanted the world to know what had really happened. The thing is you didn't find any missing persons or suspicious murders back then."

"No, we didn't. And we did a thorough search after you told us what the book was about."

Then it hit me like a rogue wave that slammed against the Irish cliffs down the road.

"Stay with me on this," I said.

"Okay." He stared at me expectantly.

"There is a lot of supposition, but what if the missing girl or boy didn't happen during their high school or college years? They'd been friends since primary school, right? That's where they all met. Maybe you need to widen your search to go back further in their history."

His eyes widened. "You think something might have happened when they were kids?"

I nodded. "It's worth checking out. And maybe you should alert the authorities in Arkansas."

"Even in the States I imagine it would take more than we have at the moment for them to exhume and test a body."

"Right. But you can at least put it out there. And can you check passports? Did one of the group go overseas to visit Keeley before her death?"

"I see where you're going with this. There's no harm to look into it."

"If we can place one of them there—maybe it will be enough for them to test Keeley's body for poisons."

"I'll see what I can do." He stood.

"I know, you need to go back to the kids. But will you let me know what you find out?"

"I will, as long as you make me a promise."

I frowned. "What's that?"

"That you won't try to interview the suspects on your own again. Sheila saw you in the pub last night. She knew exactly what you were doing. If one of them is a killer, we don't want you asking the wrong questions. This is a dangerous business, and you need to be careful. Remember what happened the last time."

I sighed. "I hear you."

"And be careful going anywhere alone. We found the tire tracks where someone tried to run the professor off the road. He told the truth about that."

"You thought he was lying?"

"No. But in my business we need definitive proof a crime has been committed. What we can't know for certain is whether that incident is related to our current case."

"Did you question him thoroughly? Maybe he doesn't realize he knows something." I'd planned to talk to him the day he'd come in disheveled into the store. "I wonder if he knows that Keeley died."

"That is something for me to find out," he said. "You've given us some new leads to follow and I thank you for that. But I'll take it from here. Stay out of it." He wagged his finger at me.

I knew he worried about me putting myself in danger, but I still rolled my eyes. Not very mature for a woman my age, but I never liked anyone telling me what to do.

My phone buzzed with a text from my sister.

"I need to head to the bookstore," I said. "Lizzie is slammed and needs someone to walk Mr. Poe."

"I'll come with you," he said.

He waited while I grabbed my coat and umbrella as the rain still fell softly. The umbrella was more to keep Mr. Poe covered as we walked. I learned the Irish way of always wearing the hood on my mac.

They had a saying here: *There's no such thing as bad weather, only bad clothing.* Or something like that. Rain and chilly winds were a part of life for those living on the coast of Ireland.

As we turned the corner onto Main Street, there were loads of little people in colorful raincoats and wellies.

"Be safe, and keep your eyes open," he said. "We're dealing with someone quite clever, and you've been asking a lot of questions."

"I will. And you'll let me know what you find out?" I asked hopefully.

"If it will keep you out of trouble, yes, I'll let you know. Though, it may take a few days to find out about the passports."

The store was packed with children, parents, and teachers. And it was much louder than normal.

"Excuse me just a moment," Lizzie said to the woman she was checking out. Then she scooped up Mr. Poe and handed him to me over the counter, along with his leash. "After his walk, do you mind taking him home? He's been such a good boy, but quite popular with the children. I sense he could use a break."

I smiled. "Of course," I said. The dog read my sister's moods well and always seemed to know exactly what she needed. But she was just as tuned in to him.

There were ooohs and awwws from people standing in line when they saw Mr. Poe. He was quite an attractive pup with his fuzzy black fur, except for his white beard and mustache. I'd named him after one of my favorite authors, and it fit. He was a friendly, talented, and mysterious little fellow who we adored.

I clipped his leash on him when we stepped outside. I swear he sighed with relief. "Okay, little dude. Do you want to visit the sea or go home?"

He cocked his head, and then tugged the leash away from the sea and up the street toward our house on the court. We had to stop every few feet so children could pet and coo over him. And he was so patient with each of them. He'd gently lick their hands and make them laugh.

He really was a superb little being. It took us nearly fifteen minutes to make the short jaunt home and I wondered if I should have gone out the back door to avoid all the adoring fans for our dog.

But as we turned the corner to head to the court, he stopped and growled. Then he barked excitedly. He'd done that before when someone had been near our door a few nights ago. I nearly tripped over him. He turned so quickly, and lunged toward the street we'd just left.

I followed his lead, but when we rounded the corner, all I could see were children with adults.

"What is it, boy?"

He continued to growl. Then he stopped and stared at me.

"Mr. Poe, I have no idea what's going on. I wish you could speak."

Still, a chill that had nothing to do with the weather slid down my spine.

"Was someone watching us?" I asked him.

He cocked his head and then yipped.

"Oh, my. You really can understand humans."

"Are they still out here?"

He stood and gazed down the street toward the sea. But before I could take a few steps in that direction, he turned and wanted to go toward home.

Whoever had been watching us was gone. But he'd sensed something. I was certain of that.

Kieran's point about staying safe hit home. I shivered again. Before stepping through the secret door that led to the court, I glanced around.

The small pathway that ran behind the Main Street stores was devoid of people.

Still, I hurried through the door.

That unsettling feeling stayed with me for hours afterward.

Someone had been watching us. And what if that was the same person who had already killed two people and possibly a third?

TWENTY-FOUR

I was grateful to have the night off. My sister had to attend a dinner held for the children's authors at the festival, but Mr. Poe and I were sequestered in front of the fire in our grandfather's private library. Even though we owned the house, it still felt like his. In a strange way, being around his books made me feel closer to him.

Before settling in, I'd checked with our neighbor Rob, who was helping with the event, and he promised to walk my sister home. I didn't want her going anywhere alone until the killer was caught.

Rob loved being involved in our mysteries and was happy to help.

Feeling good about myself because I'd knocked out three chapters and had officially hit the last third of my current work in progress, I decided to dive into research.

I paid for the privilege of a database that gave me access to old newspapers worldwide. I never used it much unless I was curious if one of the cases I made up had some hint of truth to them. More often than not, they did. At least peripherally. There truly was nothing new under the sun.

I prided myself on not using true crime events, so I'd change things up if I found too many things that were similar.

But tonight, I had a different sort of plan. If I wasn't allowed to talk to the suspects, I could at the very least find out everything about them.

I had to do some math on my phone, but figured out when they would have been in primary school, and I started with that year. I had a long way to go, but at least I had a beginning.

While I didn't find anything about the suspects in those early years, I did learn a great deal about Shamrock Cove and my grandfather. He had been very involved with the town, as well as the literary festival. Even though it had nothing to do with my investigation, I was fascinated to find out how well-respected he was.

There were even a few articles about my dad in his school soccer team. It seemed he was quite the athlete, which was something neither me, or my twin, could claim. We were both klutzes with a capital K.

When I hit upon a picture of my dad with my grandfather, tears burned in my eyes. I hadn't known either of them, but they were smiling in the picture. They stood behind the counter of the bookstore. The look on my grandfather's face as he stared down at my dad showed the love there. My dad had to be no more than six or seven. I tried to find myself in his face but there was no resemblance.

It broke my heart that they were never able to mend their relationship later in life. My poor grandfather had died without his family around. And had never known what happened to my dad after he went missing during a military mission for the government.

I hit print because I thought Lizzie would like to see the photo and the article, which was about the expansion of the second story of the bookstore. The second story had been an attic until then. It was hard to imagine the store as just one level. And he'd done such a wonderful job of making the upstairs look as beautiful and magical as the downstairs.

But it was my father's eyes that stopped me dead. They were Lizzie's gray eyes. I hadn't noticed that in the few photos we'd found. My eyes were blue and I had lighter hair. She had dark hair like our mom, but her eyes were definitely our dad's.

It was tough not to do a search on my family, but I decided we'd waited this long to hunt through records about them, so it could wait. Since we'd arrived, I'd been busy catching up on book deadlines, but I was still behind. Lizzie had been crazy slammed with the store and preparing for the festival.

I searched for James's name in chronological order so I could skip ahead.

The first article was about a writing contest. There was a picture of a group of children who were fifth graders and they stood in front of the church down the street. The article was about three of Shamrock Cove's very own young people placing in the youth writing contest at the festival. The works had been judged blindly and had included stories from children all over Ireland.

Three of the children had names I recognized—James Brandt, Keeley Boyle, and Mark Patrickson and had placed first, second, and third, respectively. As I read on, I discovered Finneas Hughes had won an honorable mention.

Wait. Chef Patrick had been a writer back then as well? And did no one think it suspicious that the friends had all placed so highly?

Maybe that was just the way my brain worked. But since they had been troublemakers later in life, I would have been trying to work out if they'd done something to sway the contest.

I wasn't sure how exactly kids could do something like that, but it was too much of a coincidence for me.

The next search was a picture of the five of them as preteens on a large sailboat. They'd been part of the regatta that took place in Shamrock Cove over the summer months.

They didn't look like a group of hoodlums. They appeared carefree and like they were having the time of their life.

But it was the next headline that stopped me and had me reading the whole article. The young teens had been questioned about a missing boy who had been seen on their boat earlier in the day.

The article stated that, though they had been questioned, the group of teens were not suspects. The article went on to say that the teens said the boy had taken a small dinghy out to sea because he'd wanted to see the whales.

Everyone believed the young man had come to a tragic end while out at sea.

But had they killed him? Was that what Keeley was trying to say in her book? And did Kieran know anything about this? He'd lived here back then, but the group had been almost ten years older.

I printed off the page.

As I went on looking through the various articles about them, a pattern emerged. They were a group of winners. Finneas had won the science fair four years in a row when he was a teen.

Keeley and James had continued to win writing awards. And Patrick won several cooking and baking contests and some were national wins.

There was an article about the teens being questioned about some missing manuscripts from the library. But the article made clear they were witnesses not suspects. The missing manuscripts were from James Joyce and C.S. Lewis.

James and his friends admitted they'd seen someone go through a window into the library when they'd been out past their curfews. But they had no idea who it was.

"And no one suspected them?"

"Suspected who?" Lizzie asked.

I screamed, and barely caught my laptop before it hit the floor.

She laughed hard.

"I'm glad you think it's funny that you scared me to death."

"What were you looking at so intensely?"

She'd be angry if I told her about the deep dive into the suspects I'd been doing. I shut my laptop quickly. "I have something to show you." I carried my computer to my office and plugged it in. Then I grabbed the first printout I'd done about our father and grandfather.

As she gazed at the picture, her hand went to her chest. "They look so happy," she whispered. "Grandad must have loved him so much."

"I agree. The look on his face says it all. Did you notice Dad's eyes? In the few photos we found, his head is always slightly turned, but this is dead on."

She frowned. "I have his eyes."

"You do."

"I wish we knew more about him. Did you find anything else?"

I cleared my throat. "Not yet."

She cocked her head. "So, tell me what you were actually researching and don't lie. I'll know."

One of the worst things about being a twin was being unable to hide things from my sister. She was right. There was no use in me trying to hide things.

"Since you and Kieran were worried about interviewing our suspects, I've been going back through their childhood and teen years."

"I think I'll need a cup of tea for this."

"Or it can wait until tomorrow. You look tired."

She was always beautiful, but her face was pale, and her eyes pulled tight at the corner.

"I won't rest until you tell me what's going on. Come on, I hid a batch of chocolate chip cookies from you. They'll go perfect with the tea."

"You hid cookies from me?"

She shrugged. "When you're writing you can eat a dozen without even thinking about it. I'm just looking out for your health. I don't want you to end up with diabetes."

She had a point.

After putting the cookies on a platter, and making ourselves some tea, we sat down with the pile of papers. I showed her what I'd found.

I didn't say anything. I wanted her to read the articles with an open mind.

Halfway through, she lifted her head. "Do you see a pattern?"

I nodded.

"And do we think they are responsible for that boy's death?"

I shrugged. "I'm beginning to think so." I told her about Keeley's book.

"Oh. My. That can't be a coincidence. Have you told Kieran yet?"

"No. It's late. I'll share what I've found with him tomorrow. He's very picky about needing proof before arresting people."

"That's so annoying." She smiled. "Why can't he just go with the assumptions we've made? Do you think one of them killed Keeley?"

"Without some sort of autopsy, we may never know. Maybe it's just that she knew she was dying. She did have a heart problem. And her last book was a way of getting truth out there about that boy."

She scrunched up her face. "Yeah, but is it a real confession if she made it fiction? And do we think she was really talking about the boy lost at sea? Even though the character in the book is a young adult woman?"

"We have no way of knowing because she's gone," I said. "But all of this is too much of a coincidence. She was dying, but the rest of them wouldn't want the information coming out. It wouldn't do any of them any favors.

"And think about it, she may be an Irish author, but she wrote for a mostly American audience. I couldn't find any of her books for sale over here."

"Let me look at something," Lizzie said as she pulled out her phone.

"What is it?"

"The catalog service we use to order books. That's odd, her novels aren't listed anywhere on here. Maybe her publisher hasn't sold the foreign rights. Not all books sell worldwide like yours."

"I'm just lucky," I said.

She cocked her head. "And a brilliant writer. By the way, I'm proud of you."

"Why is that?"

"As soon as you found out this information you didn't run and try to talk to the suspects again."

That didn't mean I wouldn't. But I'd have to be very careful when I asked the mayor, professor, and chef if they were responsible for murdering the young boy, their friends, and Sebrena.

I really didn't want to end up dead.

TWENTY-FIVE

It was the last day of the festival and I was busy helping my sister set up for the banquet in the church that was to take place that evening. It would be a final goodbye, as it was the last dinner for the attendees.

"Is it terrible that I'm ecstatic it's almost over?" Lizzie said. "I'm exhausted."

"You've been going ninety miles an hour for ten days straight, I think it's okay for you to need a break."

She laughed. "I may close the store for a few days so Caro and I can catch up on our rest."

"That's not such a bad idea." I'd been worried that she was throwing herself a bit too much into the festival to keep her mind off the past. It had been a little over a year since her fiancé and his daughter had been killed, and she was still mourning.

"Were you able to give Kieran everything you found yesterday about the chef and the mayor?" she asked. "I really hope it isn't one of them. We've been eating Chef Patrick's food all week. Makes me feel queasy to think he would have used poison."

"Or hired someone to use it."

She stopped putting the small pots of flowers in the middle of the tablecloth. "Who do you mean?"

I shrugged. "I don't know, the professor maybe. Who else would know about those kinds of poisons or how to use them? Maybe it's been Finneas all along."

She shivered. "I just wish Kieran would hurry and find whoever it is. My nerves can't take much more."

A door slammed, and I realized someone had been listening to us.

Lizzie's eyes went wide. "What if it was one of them?"

Darn. I should have been more careful.

I took off toward the door to the kitchen and she followed.

"Maybe, you should call Kieran first."

"I'm just going to peek and see if anyone is in here."

She stood right behind me as the door squeaked open.

"So much for not announcing our arrival."

Two men from the catering company were counting the glassware.

"Did you see anyone come through? We heard a door shut."

They glanced at me like I was crazy. "We're the only ones here right now. Are the tables ready to be set? The boss wanted them done early so we could focus on food prep."

Lizzie cleared her throat. "Yes."

"And was your boss in here just now?"

"Can't see how that's any business of yours, but no," one of the guys said. He wore a white T-shirt and black and white chef pants. He didn't seem to like us being in his kitchen. "It's just us."

I let go of a breath I didn't know I'd been holding. And I sensed Lizzie relaxing behind me.

"Sorry we bothered you," Lizzie said as she pulled me back.

"The church is huge," I said. "We were in the middle of the banquet room and the sound could have come from anywhere. It was probably someone who works here."

"I'm sure you're right. Still, I'd feel better if you had a chance to talk to Kieran."

"I will." In truth, I'd been waiting for him to come back from Dublin. He'd gone there to rush the postmortem reports. We—well, he—needed all the information he could get.

He'd hoped the Dublin lab would rush it since he'd lose one of his suspects once the festival was over as Chef Patrick spent most of his time at his restaurant in the city. I was anxious to share what I'd learned in my deep dive into the three men, but I wanted to do so in person.

After we finished setting up, I headed home, and Lizzie went back to the store for some signings. I'd tried to get out of going to the banquet, as I was all peopled out, but Lizzie had begged me to announce the speaker for the evening. It was impossible for me to say no to her.

I gathered all the information I had on the suspects and put them in a file. Were the three men working together? Or was one of them knocking off witnesses to his crime? Those were questions I couldn't yet answer. But even though Kieran would need more evidence, my gut seldom lied in these situations. It was one of those men.

Well, I'd sort of ruled out the professor since real tire tracks had been found near the cliff, but he still might have been unknowingly protecting the killer.

Feeling anxious, I couldn't just sit down and work. I texted Kieran to ask when he'd be back and to let him know I had information. He sent a message that he'd be home later in the evening. He was still waiting for two sets of reports.

I couldn't quite settle, so I went to the store to see how things were going. They'd just finished the last signing of the day, and the crowd had thinned in the store.

Caro and my sister were behind the counter checking out the last of the customers.

"Is everything okay?" Lizzie asked.

I nodded. "I thought Mr. Poe might like a stroll."

At the mention of his name, he sat up in his bed behind the counter, and then cocked his head. He stared at my sister and then his leash, which was on a brass hook above his bed.

We laughed.

"I think that's a yes," she said. Then her eyes narrowed. "It really is just a walk, right?"

"Yes. I'm just restless and thought I'd see if he wanted to join me."

"Okay," she said hesitantly. "Just be careful."

I smiled. "Always."

She snorted.

A few minutes later, Mr. Poe and I were headed down the hill toward the sea. He loved to chase the waves, and I enjoyed watching him do it. We were just passing the pub when Mr. Poe stopped and growled.

I turned quickly to see who was around us, but there were only a few people, and I didn't recognize any of them. A shiver slithered down my spine.

"Come on, boy, waves are waiting for you."

He let out a small bark, but then headed toward the beach.

"Don't freak me out like that," I said. "There's a killer running around town."

The rain had stopped but the wind coming off the water was still chilly. We had the beach to ourselves, so I took off his lead and let him run after the water. He was so funny as he chased the water as it receded, but was quick enough to avoid the waves when they came in. He made quite the game of it and I couldn't stop laughing.

After the stress of the last week, it felt good to relax. My shoulders dropped, and I took a deep breath of the salty air.

By the time we made it back up the hill, Lizzie had closed the shop. So, we headed home.

The water was running upstairs, so I assumed she was in the shower. After making sure Mr. Poe had food and water, I headed to my room to change. I wore a navy suit with a white silk blouse underneath, and my black boots. It was cocktail attire, so I added the diamond stud earrings my mom had given me, and a tennis bracelet I'd bought at Tiffany when I sold my second book.

While the gifts weren't always so fancy, I tried to reward myself every time I finished a novel.

I met my sister at the front door, and Mr. Poe sat blocking it.

"I believe we're headed to a pup-free zone," I said to him.

He yipped.

"He's been anxious off and on all day," she said. "If we take you, you have to sit under the table and be a very good boy."

He yipped again.

I shook my head. "You spoil him."

"He's not spoiled—he's our protector. This is his way of keeping us safe. If he thinks his presence is necessary, we should listen. Besides, no one will even know he's there. Also, I've been waiting for a chance for him to wear his new bow tie."

"Well, I guess the worst that could happen is the committee sends us home, which I wouldn't mind at all."

She laughed. "You really aren't a people person."

"You know me so well."

"Since it is Lolly who heads the committee and her Bernard will most likely be sitting on the floor beside her, I think it will be fine."

She had a point. Our neighbor Lolly had narcolepsy and her Irish Wolfhound went everywhere with her. If she fell asleep, he'd protect her until she woke up.

Bernard and Mr. Poe had become unlikely friends. They looked like Mutt and Jeff when they were together. Bernard was the size of a small pony and Mr. Poe weighed ten pounds, though you'd never know it from his attitude.

When we arrived at the banquet hall in the church, there were only a few committee members there. Our neighbors, Rob, Scott, Brenna and Lolly were among them, as was Bernard.

He and Mr. Poe sniffed one another and wagged their tails at each other. No one said a word about us bringing our dog to the banquet. This was definitely not New York.

"You did a fantastic job," Lolly said. "Everything looks so lovely. We showed up early thinking that there would be work to be done, but the staff said you'd been here earlier and had taken care of everything."

"I know how tired everyone is," Lizzie said. "Mercy and I decided to make this a fun night for you all, and a lot less work."

I had no idea that had been her plan, but I nodded.

"Well, it was kind of you," Rob interjected. "Hello, young man," he said to Mr. Poe. He and Scott knelt to pet our pup. They'd all fallen in love with him. It was impossible not to.

"I hope you don't mind," Lizzie said. "He was anxious when we tried to leave the house, so I brought him along."

"Not to worry," Lolly said. "He's your emotional support animal and is always welcome."

She wasn't wrong. Even though that wasn't an official title, Mr. Poe was a great comfort to my sister. She'd had far fewer panic attacks since he'd arrived in our lives.

The doors opened to the waiting crowd outside, and we made our way to the front table. Mr. Poe sat by Lizzie's chair as our neighbors gathered to sit down. I was grateful to my sister for putting me at a table where I already knew everyone, and I didn't have to be "on" all night for strangers.

I noticed she'd done that more than once during the festival.

She hadn't been wrong when she mentioned I was all peopled out.

Lolly went to the podium. "I want to thank all of you for

making this event so wonderful. It has been one of our more successful festivals, and as I said the other night, we've raised a record amount for our literacy charity."

Everyone clapped.

"Before we introduce our final speaker, dinner will be served. We hope you enjoy this evening, and again, I give you my sincerest thanks for helping us exceed our financial goals for the charity."

As she left the stage, the waitstaff came out with the food.

About forty-five minutes later, my sister nudged me with her elbow. It was time for me to give my introduction. I pulled up my Notes app on my phone and then made my way to the stage.

"We are so lucky to have tonight's speaker join us for our festival," I said. "Her books on recovering from trauma have helped so many, myself included."

I glanced up to find Finneas and the mayor arguing in the corner of the banquet hall. Then the mayor headed through the side door into the kitchen. The professor quickly followed.

What is all that about?

I cleared my throat. "Ladies and gentlemen, please give a warm welcome to Doctor LePerla."

Everyone stood and gave her a standing ovation. I totally understood. She really had helped give Lizzie and me perspective after our tragic losses. All through the books she had written.

But as much as I wanted to listen to what she had to say, I was pulled toward that kitchen door by instinct.

When I pushed it open, my heart jumped into my throat.

I should have gone back to my table.

TWENTY-SIX

The waitstaff, along with the mayor and the professor, huddled in a corner of the industrial kitchen. Near the stove was Chef Patrick, pointing a very scary shotgun at the small crowd.

"Get in here," he growled.

Well, darn. I had not seen this coming. I mean, I knew it had to be one of the three, but he was the least likely of my choices. My stomach twisted into knots. I'd walked straight into the lion's den.

I started to head toward those in the corner, but he motioned me to come near him. My legs turned to Jell-O, and it was all I could do to walk the few feet to where he stood.

Everything in me screamed for me to run, but he was too close with that gun.

"You cannot kill us all," the mayor said calmly. "Just put the gun down, and we can talk about this."

"We aren't chums," the chef growled again. Anger came off him in waves as he grabbed my arm, and then put the gun at my back. "You and Finneas know it was me. If any of you make a move, I'll shoot her and then you."

I swallowed the bile that crawled to my throat.

"If you're going to kill me, can you at least tell me why you murdered your ex-wife Sebrena and James?"

"Isn't that obvious? She cheated on me with my best friend and these two knew all along. They made me look like an idiot. They all deserve to die."

Wait. This had nothing to do with the missing boy or manuscript? I mean, part of me was disappointed that it had boiled down to jealousy. The other part of me was quite concerned I might not survive this encounter.

"Friends tell one another when they are married to a cheating harpy. And James, he was never happy unless he had whatever I did. After all these years of protecting him from his sordid past, he took my Sebrena."

I'd met the woman and I would have said James did him a favor but now was not the time to say so. I never liked it when men saw other humans as their possessions, but that was something else I planned to keep to myself.

"I'm telling you we had no idea," the mayor said.

"You went out with them. I saw the photos on her phone. You and Finneas were in the photos. They were dated long before she left me for him. I'm always cleaning up after you guys, and then you couldn't be bothered to tell me about them."

"But wasn't that years ago?" I asked. I couldn't help myself. Besides, as long as he was talking, maybe he wouldn't kill me.

"You nosing around hasn't helped matters. If you'd left things alone, the police wouldn't suspect any of us. It took me time to plan everything and to bide my time until an opportunity arose."

My stomach churned, and it really was all I could do to keep my food down.

"All of this because you were angry at James and Sebrena?" I asked. "Did you also kill Keeley?"

"No. She's dead?" He was behind me but sounded perplexed.

"Yes," I said shakily.

"I'd nothing to do with that. I loved Keeley like a sister."

"Even though she told the truth about the missing boy you guys killed on your sailboat?"

He shoved the gun in my back. "I've no idea what you're talking about."

"Her latest book was a fictionalized version of the boy you all killed when you were teens." I had to keep him talking, and I prayed someone would notice I was gone from the main hall.

"That had nothing to do with me, and everything to do with your good mayor."

"It was an accident," the mayor said, wide-eyed. "And we were protecting each other."

"That's another mess I cleaned up for you," Chef Patrick said. "I took the dinghy out and swum back so your story would hold true. And how do you pay me back? By letting that jerk take my Sebrena."

This was a really messed-up situation.

He stabbed the nozzle of the gun harder into my back. I had to do something.

I'm going to die. Poor Lizzie will be all alone.

No. I couldn't let that happen.

I glanced around for some kind of weapon, but all of the knives were too far away.

Just as I was about to give up my search, the door to the kitchen opened and three things happened at once.

"Are you hiding in here?" Lizzie asked. At the same time, Mr. Poe quickly assessed the situation and ran in, grabbed the chef's leg and bit down hard. I turned and grabbed an iron skillet off the stove. Thankfully it wasn't hot. Then I swung with all my might.

The shotgun clattered to the floor, and the chef swayed back and forth before doing a face-plant.

I hoped I hadn't killed him, but I quickly grabbed the gun so none of his so-called friends could pick it up.

The group in the corner started to move toward us but I shook my head.

"Everyone stay where you are. The police will need to gather evidence and speak to all of you."

"You cannot tell us what to do," the mayor said.

"Oh, stuff it," the professor said. "You will no longer be mayor after all this. Do what you must," he said to me.

"Lizzie, call the police and tell them it's an emergency."

Since there were extra police as security for the festival, the place was soon swarming with officers. Kieran showed up about fifteen minutes later, having just come back to town.

He looked from me to the man on the floor. He still wasn't awake, and the EMTs were treating him. At least he was alive, there was that.

I sat on the counter near the stove as my legs had finally given out.

"I see you've been busy," he said. His eyebrows went up.

"Wrong place, wrong time," I said.

He chuckled. "You make a habit of that."

"You aren't wrong," Lizzie said from beside me on the counter. She held Mr. Poe in her lap.

"You're both white as sheets, why don't you head home. I'll come by and get your statements later."

We nodded in unison.

I left the scene on wobbly legs, I don't think Lizzie was feeling much better, but with the help of Rob and Scott she held me up. At home, Mr. Poe went to the back door and she let him out.

"Sit down, and I'll make you a cup of tea."

"Cookies will be helpful. I missed dessert."

She shook her head. "You ate all the cookies."

Rob and Scott laughed as they sat down at the table.

"I have some scones I made for tomorrow's breakfast," Lizzie said.

"Those will do."

We sat there in silence and sipped our tea.

"What made you go in there?" Rob asked.

I explained what I'd seen while doing my introduction.

"You could have been killed," Lizzie said. A tear slid down her cheek. I reached across the table and took her hand in mine.

"I'm sorry I scared you. I was just curious as to why they were arguing. I had no idea he had a gun."

"You know, it was you and Mr. Poe who saved the day. If you hadn't distracted him right then, things might have been much worse."

She shivered. "I don't want to think about that."

Neither did I. That had been a close one. My stomach still twirled with nerves, and it was all I could do to keep the tea down.

It was late when Kieran showed up at the house.

"He's regained consciousness," he said. "He'll be seen for his injuries, but you needn't worry. He's under police custody and will not be going anywhere but jail."

"What about the mayor and the professor?" I asked.

"Also under police caution, they will not be going anywhere. My superiors insisted they be held and charged in Dublin." He pulled out his pen and tablet. He also put a recorder on the table. "Take me through everything as it happened."

"Please have a scone," Lizzie said. "I'll get you some tea, unless you need something stronger."

"Tea will be grand," he said.

I told him everything that happened. "The mayor and

Finneas helped cover up the missing boy's death. Well, with Patrick's help."

"Aye, we're aware. The professor, who was hoping for a lighter sentence, confessed everything. Even if it was an accident, they will be tried for covering it up. Oh, and it was the mayor who stole Keeley's early manuscript from your home."

"The mayor?" I asked, shocked.

"Aye. When he asked for a report on the case, I'd mentioned the book. He'd asked Finneas to be the lookout but he'd taken off when he saw your sister coming."

"So, the boy in the boat *had* been the big cover-up. She'd just changed it to a woman in that early draft."

"That's what we think. Since she died, we cannot ask her," he said.

"That explains why Patrick tried to kill the professor as well. I guess in time he would have gone after the mayor as well."

Kieran nodded. "He'd been expecting quid pro quo is my guess. We'll know more when we formally interview him."

When we were done, he shook his head.

"You two have a penchant for trouble."

"I blame her." Lizzie pointed at me. "Her timing never has been particularly great."

"Thanks a lot. But we caught the killer and two men acting in collusion for another death. I believe the words you're looking for are, 'thank you.'"

Kieran chuckled.

"Quick thinking with the pan," he said.

"It honestly happened so fast I don't even remember thinking about it. I acted on sheer instinct." I rubbed my shoulder. "It was a very heavy pan."

"Well, that worked in your favor and probably saved your life. I suppose you'll be wanting to listen in when we question him tomorrow. Provided he's recovered enough from his injuries."

I bit my lip. "Is it too much to ask?"

"No. You deserve answers as much as anyone. Now, you two go get some rest." He put his hand on my shoulder, and warmth spread through me.

Then he was gone.

After everything that had happened, I wasn't sure how I would fall asleep.

I was more than curious about what Chef Patrick would have to say for himself.

TWENTY-SEVEN

The next day I sat in Kieran's office extremely disappointed. He had let me watch on a video link, but I wasn't allowed in the room itself. As soon as they started questioning him, Chef Patrick, whose head was bandaged, told them everything. His solicitor had encouraged him to come clean since there had been so many witnesses to his confession in the kitchen.

Word for word it was what I'd given in my statement the night before.

Then Kieran asked the question that hadn't been answered.

"You said you still loved Sebrena," Kieran said. "Then why did you poison her like you did James?"

"She'd seen me at the cottage the night before," he said. "Or at least, she thought it was me on the motorcycle. She confronted me. I told her she was nuts, but I couldn't have her talking to you. It would have ruined everything."

"But when did you poison her?"

"We had a banquet service for breakfast that day. I slipped it into her tea. It took a while to work. I made sure I was the one who cleared the service and disposed of the cup. I thought it would kill her there.

"No one was more surprised than me when she got up and walked away. Constitution of a horse, that one. I'd found the poison while researching herbs for one of my dishes more than a year ago. I couldn't believe my luck when the literary committee accepted my catering bid. Everything fell into place after that."

"And did you cause the blackout at the time of James Brandt's murder?"

"No. Had nothing to do with it. I was already leaving the cottage. He had no idea I'd poisoned him. He was angry with me for bringing Keeley's manuscript that she'd left with me when she went to America, especially when I told him she'd just published it in the States. He then threw me out."

"I think I know what happened," I said to my sister, who was sitting next to me in Kieran's office.

"What?"

"It never made sense why James pulled the bookcase down on himself. But he must have been stumbling around in the dark as he was dying. When he tried to steady himself, he pulled the bookcase down."

"That's awful," she said.

"It is. Especially if he didn't die right away."

We shivered.

"Did you help cover up the death of Doctor Hughes's wife?" Kieran asked.

That had come out of the blue, and I wondered if he'd found some tie to her death and what had been going on the past week.

"No," he said. "Finn loved his wife. He wouldn't have hurt her."

"Well, I guess that's it," I said to Lizzie.

My sister laughed. "You seem disappointed. Aren't you glad he confessed?"

"It really isn't like on television or the movies."

"Well, you heard what Kieran said. The cards were already

stacked against him. The court will consider his willingness to confess when his sentence is decided. Do they have the death penalty in Ireland?" she asked.

"No. Not for a couple of decades."

"Oh. I was just curious about what he might be facing."

"Kieran said at least one lifetime in prison, possibly two. He said we had no worries of him ever getting out."

Her phone buzzed, and she smiled.

"Who is it?"

"Rob and Scott. They want to know what's happening. They're making us lunch. Lolly and Brenna will be there as well."

I wasn't surprised. Our neighbors on the court looked out for one another. Actually, all of Shamrock Cove did. It was one of the reasons we loved our new town so much. The people genuinely cared for one another.

"I can't imagine this will go on much longer," I said. "I've heard enough."

She appeared surprised.

"What?" I asked.

"I figured you'd want to sit here to the very end."

"Tell them we will be there shortly."

A half-hour later, I'd told them everything about what we'd heard over plates of what Rob called Irish comfort food: corned beef, delightfully light mashed potatoes, and several other sides. Mom would have called it stick-to-your-ribs kind of food.

"Thank goodness for your instincts," Lolly said. "My grandson says your quick thinking saved the day."

I shrugged. "I guess all that researching and martial arts training pays off when it counts."

"It does," Lizzie said.

There was a small yip from under the table.

"And Mr. Poe's quick biting," I added.

Mr. Poe was snuggled between Lizzie and me. Though he never begged, she would feed him the occasional morsel of meat. After all, he had saved me from a killer.

I loved this place and our friends. Life in Shamrock Cove was good and I would never again take it for granted.

My phone buzzed. It was a text from Carrie.

Okay, big hero. That book better be on time. And thank God you are alive. Stop scaring me like that.

I laughed. Lizzie asked who it was and I told them.

Everyone around the table smiled.

Yes, life was good. And I was more than grateful to be surrounded by our new friends.

But now that I had the crime-solving bug, I wondered when the next mystery might come to Shamrock Cove.

A LETTER FROM LUCY CONNELLY

Lovely reader,

I want to say a huge thank you for choosing to read *Death by the Book*. If you did enjoy it, and want to keep up to date with all my latest releases, just sign up at the following link. Your email address will never be shared, and you can unsubscribe anytime.

www.bookouture.com/lucy-connelly

One of the things I loved about writing *Death by the Book* was being transported to Ireland and Shamrock Cove, and a book festival that I would love to attend. How about you? And what do you think of the twins, Mercy and Lizzie? I love the town and how the twins are settling in there.

I'd love to hear what you think, and it makes such a difference helping new readers to discover one of my books for the first time if you write a review.

I love hearing from my readers—you can get in touch through my social media or my website.

Love to you all,

Lucy Connelly

KEEP IN TOUCH WITH LUCY

www.lucyconnelly.com

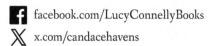 facebook.com/LucyConnellyBooks

x.com/candacehavens

ACKNOWLEDGMENTS

I want to thank the amazing team at Bookouture for being such wonderful partners in making this book happen. A big shout-out to my editor, Maisie, for her incredible insights.

Jill Marsal, thank you for your guidance and support throughout the years. I couldn't do this without you.

It takes a village for Lucy to write a book, and I couldn't have done it without the love and support of my family and friends.

Last but not least, thank you, dear readers, for picking up these books and for joining me on the journey. You have no idea how much your kind words mean to me.

PUBLISHING TEAM

Turning a manuscript into a book requires the efforts of many people. The publishing team at Bookouture would like to acknowledge everyone who contributed to this publication.

Audio
Alba Proko
Sinead O'Connor
Melissa Tran

Commercial
Lauren Morrissette
Hannah Richmond
Imogen Allport

Cover design
Lisa Horton

Data and analysis
Mark Alder
Mohamed Bussuri

Editorial
Maisie Lawrence
Sinead O'Connor

Printed in the USA
CPSIA information can be obtained
at www.ICGtesting.com
LVHW091458081124
796093LV00004B/44